LUKE SUTTON: LAWMAN

Also by Leo P. Kelley

LUKE SUTTON: LAWMAN

LEO P. KELLEY

A Double D Western Book

Doubleday

NEW YORK   LONDON   TORONTO   SYDNEY   AUCKLAND

All of the characters in this book are fictitious,
and any resemblance to actual persons, living or
dead, is purely coincidental.

A Double D Western Book

Published by Doubleday, a division of
Bantam Doubleday Dell Publishing Group, Inc.
666 Fifth Avenue, New York, New York 10103

Double D, Doubleday, and the portayal of the
letters DD are trademarks of Doubleday, a division of
Bantam Doubleday Dell Publishing Group, Inc.

Library of Congress Cataloging-in-Publication Data

Kelley, Leo P.
Luke Sutton, lawman / Leo P. Kelley. — 1st ed.
p.   cm.—(A Double D western)
I. Title.
PS3561.E388L837   1989   88-17551
813'.54—dc19   CIP

ISBN 0-385-24185-2
Copyright © 1989 by Leo P. Kelley
All Rights Reserved
Printed in the United States of America
March 1989
First Edition

LUKE SUTTON: LAWMAN

ONE

As Luke Sutton stepped out of the front door of Virginia City's International Hotel, the omnipresent wind that was always tearing down the slopes of Mount Davidson struck him and almost ripped the black Stetson from his head.

But he caught his hat in time and held on to it as he made his way down C Street past Chinese peddlers with their baskets of fruit hung from long poles balanced on their shoulders and men with coal-dust-blackened faces just up from the mines and looking like Satan's own imps.

He stopped for a few minutes to join the crowd that was gathered around an organ-grinder whose emaciated monkey was dressed in a tiny red jacket and a tinier red fez. It darted among the forest of people's legs, its tin cup held up beseechingly, its black eyes blinking rapidly, its free paw vigorously scratching its flea-infested fur.

As coins clinked their way into the monkey's tin cup, the organ-grinder, a mustachioed man who huffed and puffed as he cranked the handle of his instrument, made a thin music that sounded more like the ghost of a tune than the tune itself. The music eased out into the air which was, as always in Virginia City, filled with swirling smoke and clouds of alkali dust blown about by the restless wind.

As a fondly smiling young woman reached down to

pet the monkey, Sutton seized her wrist and pulled her hand back just as the monkey, still scratching and still proffering its tin cup, bared its yellow teeth and snapped at the woman's hand that was no longer there, thanks to Sutton.

"Oh!" the woman cried in alarm. She drew back, turned to Sutton, and said, "Thank you, sir, for saving me from that savage little monster."

He touched the brim of his hat to her and left the crowd. As he continued walking down C Street, his rolling gait identified him as a horseman, a man more comfortable in the saddle than on foot. The way his gunmetal gray eyes moved restlessly from side to side, taking in everything around him, defined him as a man who knew that it was wise to walk warily through a world that was full of surprises, not all of them pleasant by any means.

Sutton was a tall man, a lean-limbed and rangy man with slight hollows beneath his cheekbones, a square jaw, thin lips and nose, and a broad forehead. His shoulders were broad and heavily muscled. His chest was thick and his hips were narrow. His long legs were strong and sinewy, his hands large but in no way ungainly.

He wore a white shirt with a paper collar beneath a black sack coat and black trousers tucked into low-heeled army boots. His string tie fluttered in the wind, as did his equally black hair that cascaded down to bury the nape of his neck and his ears, which lay flat against the side of his head.

He continued walking along C Street, touching the brim of his hat to women along the way who greeted him and stopping briefly at one point to exchange pleasantries with a man named Henry Stilling who was, as he was, a volunteer fireman with Virginia City's Engine Company Number Four.

When he reached his destination—the Fourth Ward School at the upper end of C Street—he went inside to find a number of men lining a long hall that led to the school's auditorium. The eyes of the men abandoned Sutton and shifted to the young woman carrying something covered in newspapers in both hands, who had entered the building moments after he did. He recognized one of the men and went over to William Wright, the editor of Virginia City's newspaper, *The Territorial Enterprise.*

"Howdy, Bill. How've you been keeping since I last laid eyes on you?"

"Very well, Luke, thank you. Yourself?"

"Can't complain. Though I will confess to feeling a bit fiddlefooted of late."

"You never light in one place for long, do you, Luke? Why it was only the other day that you got back from your most recent manhunt. By the way, Aaron Endicott and Violet Wilson are planning on naming the day, did you know?"

"No, I didn't. But when I finally ran Endicott down for Miss Wilson it was clear to me that she would teach him to stand hitched before too long."

"And now you say you want to be on the move again? So soon?"

"I'm not a man who takes kindly to staying put, Bill. I have to be on the move. If I'm not, I start to rust."

Wright shook his head in mock consternation. "Being on the move is one thing. Getting shot at as you have been too often of late is quite another."

Sutton grinned and clapped Wright on the back. "Getting shot at now and then does wonders for keeping a man on his toes. Speaking of keeping on one's toes, where are all the women? I don't see a single filly of either the claimed or unclaimed variety. Is this shindig going to turn out to be a bachelor party? If so, I'll be on my merry way."

"The ladies," Wright said, "are all in the auditorium setting things up. The men, as you can see, are all lined up out here while they try to figure out which lady is bringing which box to the box supper tonight so they can be sure they're bidding on the box belonging to the lady of their choice when the auction starts."

"Speaking of choice ladies—" Sutton nudged Wright in the ribs and indicated the young woman who had just come in the door with something in her hands that was covered by a fringed shawl. "Who might she be?"

The woman Sutton had indicated was almost as tall as he was, partly because her red hair was elaborately done up and piled high on her head. Her eyes were a striking blue and her complexion was creamy. Her fine-boned face was one of classical beauty, and her graceful carriage lent her an air of quiet elegance.

"Miss Letitia Parsons," Wright said.

"I thought I knew all the good-looking women between here and Gold Hill. Is she new in town?"

"Miss Parsons moved here recently from Carson City," Wright answered. "Would you like to meet her?"

"Bill, asking me that's like asking does a cat like lapping cream. Come on. Introduce me to Miss Parsons before she gets away."

Miss Parsons, who had stopped to chat with one of the men in the hall, began moving toward the auditorium. Sutton grabbed Wright's arm and hurried him down the hall after her. When they had caught up with their quarry, Wright said, "Good evening, Miss Parsons."

"Oh, Mr. Wright," she responded pleasantly. "How nice to see you again. I have been meaning to come into your office to tell you how very pleased I am with the advertisements you prepared for me. They have done wonders for my business."

"I am always glad to hear such kind words from one of the *Enterprise*'s advertisers," Wright responded. "We do our best to produce the best possible advertisements —and news reports—for our readers."

"I hope you won't think me unkind, Mr. Wright, but I must say if that is the case I think you would do well not to run such stories as those about that young murderer which recently appeared in your pages."

"You are referring to our coverage of the Jimmy Lee Cranston trial, I take it?"

"Yes, I am. That was a terrible thing he did and for one so young to be a killer—it makes me shudder every time I think of it. I wish you wouldn't carry such stories, Mr. Wright. Oh, I know they are news. But surely people would be better off if they didn't have to read about such awful things."

"You are clearly a woman of delicate sensibilities, Miss Parsons," Wright said. "But I must tell you that most people are nowhere nearly as refined as you yourself so obviously are. Most of our readers, sad to say, dote on such stories as the murder of Seth Grant by Jimmy Lee Cranston. The circulation of the *Enterprise* soared during our coverage of the Cranston trial."

Miss Parsons sighed. "I'm sure what you say is true, Mr. Wright, which is certainly a sad commentary on the public's taste, in my humble opinion."

Before Wright could say anything more, Sutton

poked him in the ribs. Wright, seeing the grimace on Sutton's face, nodded and said, "Miss Parsons, may I introduce you to a very good friend of mine, Mr. Lucas Sutton. Luke, may I present Miss Letitia Parsons, who owns and operates a ribbon shop here in town. Perhaps you have seen the advertisements for her shop which appear from time to time in our newspaper."

Miss Parsons turned her blue eyes, which seemed to Sutton to blaze, upon him and held out her hand. He took it, bent, kissed it. "It's a pleasure to make your acquaintance, Miss Parsons," he said, hypnotized by her steady gaze and close to being stunned by her beauty.

"How do you do, Mr. Sutton?"

"The best I can," he answered. "Is that a box supper you've got there?"

"Why, yes, it is."

"I reckon it will bring a pretty price. In fact, it ought to rake in enough money to fund at least one of the teacher's salaries for the whole of the next school year."

"It's nice of you to say so, Mr. Sutton." Turning to Wright, Miss Parsons asked, "Are all of your gentleman friends such flatterers?"

"I'm afraid most of them are," Wright admitted with a smile. And then he added, "But none of them have the facility that Luke has in kissing the hand of a lady as if he had been born and bred in Paris, France."

"Learned how to do that from a riverboat gambler a long time ago," Sutton said with a smile.

"You sound like a man with a past, Mr. Sutton," Miss Parsons commented.

"He definitely won't have much of a future," Wright interjected, "if he keeps practicing his very dangerous profession of tracking down desperate men and women who do not want to be tracked down."

Miss Parsons' lips parted. "Luke Sutton," she breathed in a voice that was little louder than an awed whisper. "I didn't recognize the name at first. But I have been reading about your exploits in Mr. Wright's newspaper, Mr. Sutton. They sounded most exciting."

"Bill here tends to blow things way out of proportion," Sutton declared. "It helps him sell his newspapers."

"I'm sure you're being unduly modest, Mr. Sutton," Miss Parsons remarked. "Now, if you gentlemen will excuse me—"

Sutton, as Miss Parsons began to move away, bumped into her. She cried out in mild alarm as she tried to keep the shawl-draped box supper in her hands from falling to the floor.

"I'm real sorry about being so clumsy," Sutton hastily told her as he helped her steady the box in her hands.

Miss Parsons gave him a smile and then hurried away down the hall.

"She must have suitors lined up outside her door every day, not to mention night," Sutton said.

"A decidedly attractive woman," Wright commented admiringly.

"I'm glad you're married, Bill," Sutton told him, "and so no competition for me where Miss Parsons is concerned."

"Shall we go in, Luke? It's almost six-thirty—time for the auction of the ladies' box suppers to begin."

Sutton and Wright joined the throng of men who were pushing their way into the auditorium. Once inside the large room, they took up strategic positions at its rear in direct line with the stage at the far end of the auditorium. On the stage rested a large table upon which in turn were countless boxes, all of them more or less gaily decorated.

"I'm here to cover this box supper for the newspaper," Wright remarked, "but you, Luke, are you here to place a bid or two?"

"I intend to bid on Miss Parsons' box supper, Bill," Sutton announced as he scanned the boxes on the table in the front of the auditorium.

"Have you been to box suppers before, Luke?"

"A whole bunch of them ever since I was a tad and more interested in tying cans to dogs' tails than to keeping company with a lady over her box supper."

"Then you know it can be a problem guessing which box belongs to which lady."

"I know which one belongs to Miss Parsons," Sutton declared confidently.

"How can you be so sure that you know hers from all the others? I certainly don't."

"I'm betting that one right there in the middle belongs to her."

"Which one?"

"The one that's wrapped in white tissue paper. The one with all those yellow ribbons on it."

"I didn't catch so much as a glimpse of the box she had hidden under that shawl of hers. What makes you so sure that one is hers?"

"You recollect how I bumped into her when she was leaving us?"

Wright nodded.

"Well, that was done accidental-on-purpose, if you take my meaning. I wanted to get to touch her box while I was pretending to be helping her hang on to it and not drop it. That's how I know it was wrapped in tissue paper—from touching it when I bumped into her."

"I see. But could you tell by the feel of the box that it was wrapped in *white* tissue paper?"

"No, but—"

"There are at least three boxes I can see from here that are wrapped in tissue paper. One in green, one in lavender, and one in white."

Sutton pulled thoughtfully at his chin. "But there's none other up there that's got yellow ribbons on it, and since Miss Parsons runs a ribbon shop here in town I reckon that one has got to be hers—the one decorated with ribbons *and* wrapped in tissue paper."

"You say you have attended box suppers before, Luke. I therefore assume you know the many kinds of ruses some women will resort to in order to keep their boxes from being identified. I myself recall one such box supper I attended where the prettiest single girl in town persuaded an older woman to carry her box in for her so that all her lovelorn swains outside would think that the box the older woman was carrying was her own and not the box belonging to the girl of all their rowdy dreams."

"Miss Parsons was carrying her own box," Sutton said firmly. "She didn't give it to some other woman to bring in for her."

"How do you know the box she was carrying was her own?"

"On account of she said it was when I asked her about it."

Wright wagged a chiding finger in front of Sutton's face. "You asked her if that was a box supper she was carrying and she said it was. You didn't ask her if that was *her* box supper she was carrying."

"I stand corrected," a chagrined Sutton muttered.

"There is another matter to consider in this question of does or does not Miss Parsons have a box supper on that table and, if she does, which one it is."

"What other matter?"

"Maybe Miss Parsons has a beau and has told that most fortunate fellow how her box will be decorated so that he may be sure to bid on the one he wants rather than on any other."

"If she does have a beau," Sutton declared firmly, "I'll outbid him." He pulled his poke from his pocket and quickly counted the money in it.

"Ladies and gents, may I have your attention?" called out a man who had mounted the stage and was standing behind the table on which the box suppers rested. "Now that I see I have your attention, folks, let me welcome you, each and every one, to our box supper which most of you no doubt know is being held to raise funds for the Fourth Ward School.

"You gents out there, you keep that important fact right up there in the forefront of your minds. If you do, I'm sure you will be generous in your bidding, not to mention enthusiastic. Bid often, gents, and bid high. If you lose out, try again—and again and yet again. This here's a fine chance for you to keep company with one of Virginia City's belles—and remember this. If you don't get the box belonging to the lady of your choice, think positive and view the box your winning bid does take as a ticket to getting to know another woman, a situation fraught with virtually all kinds of possibilities and—"

"Hiram," shouted a man in the crowd, "get on with it, will you, before the first snow starts falling!"

Hiram ignored the outburst. "Now, what about this

box here, gents?" He held up one that had a red paper rose fastened to its top. "Would you believe me if I told you the supper inside this box was put up by someone who happens to live on D Street and has a dimple in her chin?"

A man next to Sutton whispered to the man next to him, "Do you believe him, Sid? Is that Betty James' box, do you really reckon? Betty James lives on D Street sure enough and she's got a dimple in her chin that's about as deep as the Silver Star's mine shaft."

Sutton didn't hear the reply to the man's question, but he knew that most box supper auctioneers were not above pulling the legs of the men in the audience to see what interesting couplings would result from the outright lies, not to mention the mild deceptions, they presented during their spiels.

"I'll tell you gents in the strictest confidence"—continued the auctioneer and a laugh rippled through the crowd—"that this box"—he held up one that was covered with crocheting—"belongs to a lady whose first name begins with the letter 'S' and that 'S' doesn't stand for Sarah."

"Sadie Jenkins," boomed a boisterous man in the crowd.

"Maybe so," said the auctioneer, "and then again it could belong to somebody named Samantha." He winked at the crowd.

Then he picked up a box, held it high above his head in one hand and said, "We'll start tonight with the 'married' boxes. These will have names, not numbers like the 'unmarried' boxes. I have here in my hand the box supper put up by the loving and capable hands of Mrs. Ken Hampton. Come on now, Ken. Let's hear what you are willing to bid for this labor of love that's been put up by your better half."

Mrs. Hampton's box was sold to her husband for one dollar and Mr. Hampton received the applause of the audience for his generous bid.

When all the "married" boxes had been auctioned off, the auctioneer held up the first of what he called the "bachelor" suppers.

"All a gent gets for one of these 'bachelor' suppers," he declared, "is the supper itself. No female companionship goes along with it. So you gents who are here only because you're hungry—for food, I mean—now it's your turn. What am I bid for this box supper?"

The bidding opened at fifty cents, went quickly to eighty, and closed at ninety-five.

Sutton waited impatiently through the auctioning of the remaining "bachelor" boxes, which the high bidders took to the tables that had been set up along the walls. There they proceeded to unpack and devour their contents. Beside Sutton, Wright made notes of names and bid prices in the little notebook he always carried, apparently unmindful of the children scampering and screaming here and there throughout the auditorium as they played tag and other raucous games.

At last, the auctioneer held up the first of the "unmarried" boxes. He asked for an opening bid.

"One dollar," from a blushing young man in the crowd.

"One dollar and ten cents," from another bidder.

A little later, the box went to the still-blushing first bidder for two dollars and five cents and the auctioneer called out the name of the person who had packed the box, which was on a slip of paper pasted on the bottom of the box.

The successful bidder leaped to his feet, paid the auctioneer two dollars and five cents and claimed both the box and the demure young woman who had packed it. Sutton watched the pair make their way, hand in hand, to one of the tables along the walls. He shifted position as more boxes came on the block and were bought with bids ranging from two dollars to nearly ten, the latter price the result of a fierce bidding war between two determined young men.

When the box that he believed to be Letitia Parsons' came up for bid twenty minutes later, Sutton was ready. His eyes flicked from the box in the auctioneer's hand to Miss Parsons, and he thought he saw her smile shyly at the woman standing beside her when the auctioneer commented on "all the fancy yellow doodads" decorating the top of the box.

Sutton didn't bid immediately but waited for several other bids to be placed, noting who was placing them and how eager the bidders seemed to be.

Wright nudged Sutton. "Luke, do you know who that wild-eyed fellow with the torn ear is who's bidding on that box Hiram's holding up?"

"I know him. Not personally but by reputation I know him. That's Kernie Bates. I know he fancies himself a bad man. Been in a couple of gunfights here in town which is how he got his ear split. From what I hear though he's more bluster than guts."

"That may be so but the point I want to make is I don't think Miss Parsons—if that is indeed her box supper Hiram's got on the block, as you seem to be so sure it is—would relish sharing it with the likes of Kernie Bates."

"I've no intention of letting Bates get his paws on it," Sutton stated and then called out, "Five dollars!" topping the previous bid, which was not Bates', by one dollar.

He didn't miss the fact that Miss Parsons, standing off to his left and slightly in front of him, turned her head to see who had placed the five-dollar bid. It's her box, he told himself. Sure as shooting it is.

Bates bid six dollars. His former opponent was silent. Bates began to grin.

He stopped grinning when Sutton bid eight dollars.

Bates promptly bid eight-fifty.

The auctioneer pointed the index finger of his free hand at Sutton and said, "I have eight-fifty, will you make it nine, sir?"

"Ten," Sutton said and the auctioneer whooped in delight, almost dropping the box held high in his right hand. "This here, folks, is turning into a true battle of the titans," he announced happily. "Kernie, you heard the man's bid. The gentleman with the glint in his eyes back there in the rear of the room has bid ten dollars. What are you going to do about that, Kernie?"

"Nothing," Sutton said under his breath, hoping.

"Don't be too sure," Wright cautioned him.

"Bates is about broke by now or I miss my guess," Sutton muttered. "If he weren't he would have topped my bid by more than a mere fifty cents his last time out."

Suddenly, Bates bid. "Ten-fifty."

"Might as well end this foolishness once and for all," Sutton said and called out, "Fifteen dollars!"

Bates glared at him but he didn't make another bid.

The auctioneer tried coaxing Bates to top Sutton's bid but Bates remained sullenly silent. "Fifteen once," the auctioneer intoned gleefully. "Fifteen twice—

Kernie, I reckon you've been beaten by a better bidder, not to mention an obviously well-heeled one."

Bates swore, causing the auctioneer to admonish him in front of the crowd and to advise him to learn to be a good loser.

"Sold for fifteen dollars," the auctioneer announced and held the box above his head to read the name on the piece of paper pasted to its bottom. "This box supper, I can tell you, folks, will prove to have inside it as delectable things as it has delightful decorations on the outside. I say that with complete confidence because this box belongs to none other than to Miss—" The auctioneer squinted at the small slip of paper in his hand, pretending he couldn't make out the name, although everyone in the room knew that he was doing nothing more than prolonging the suspense before revealing the identity of the owner of the box supper Sutton had just won with his high bid.

"Miss Letitia Parsons!" the auctioneer called out at last.

"You did it!" Wright crowed and clapped Sutton on the back.

"Didn't I just!" responded a delighted Sutton as he made his way through the crowd to claim his prize.

After handing the auctioneer fifteen dollars, he took the box from the man and made his way back to where Letitia Parsons was standing.

When he reached her, he said, "I hope you don't mind that it was me who had the high bid on this here." He indicated the box in his hand.

"On the contrary, Mr. Sutton, I am pleased that you were the successful bidder and quite flattered that you were so generous with your bids. The school fund will be all the richer for the price you paid for my box supper."

"I'm no philanthropist, Miss Parsons. I wasn't bidding to enrich the school fund but to make sure I was the one who got to share your supper."

"I hope you like cold lamb and peach preserves, Mr. Sutton."

"Let's sit down right here, Miss Parsons." Sutton pulled a chair out from a table, and after he had seated Miss Parsons, he sat down across from her and handed her the box supper. "Will you do the honors?"

Before she could take the box from him, a shadow fell across the table. Sutton looked up to see Kernie Bates glaring down at him.

Bates said, "Just because you're a rich so-and-so that don't make it fair what you just went and did."

"What I just did, Bates," Sutton said coldly, "was to bid fair and square on this box supper." He turned his attention back to Miss Parsons who was gazing apprehensively at the looming Bates.

"I may not have the kind of money you've got," Bates growled at Sutton, "but what I have got is the guts to take that box supper and the lady, too, away from you."

"I'm not hankering after trouble, Bates," Sutton said, "so why don't you just go back where you came from and leave us be?"

"It's you that's moving out," Bates snarled, "and leaving me and the lady be. Now *git!*"

"Miss Parsons," Sutton said quietly, "would you prefer the company of this fellow to mine? If you would, I'll oblige you and make myself scarce."

"No, don't do that, Mr. Sutton, please don't," Miss Parsons pleaded.

Sutton looked up at Bates and said, "You heard the

lady. She's made her wishes plain where you and me's concerned."

Bates reached down and made a grab for Sutton, who ducked to one side, avoiding the man's grasping hands. In an instant, Sutton was up, his chair toppling to the floor behind him, and squaring off against Bates who, he noted, had a good twenty-pound advantage over him and who topped him by a good two to three inches.

"You can git," Bates told Sutton, "while the gitting's still good. You do and I won't have to wipe up the floor with you."

"I don't aim to git," Sutton said, "so if knuckle and skull's the way you want it, let's have at it."

Bates lunged at Sutton, one hairy fist raised and sledgehammering its way through the air toward Sutton's jaw.

Sutton nimbly sidestepped the bony weapon, then knocked it to one side and delivered a roundhouse right that caused Bates to gasp and momentarily back off. But then Bates let out a grunt and went for Sutton again. This time he landed a left on Sutton's shoulder and a right on his chest.

Sutton countered with a left jab that glanced off Bates' cheekbone and left Sutton's knuckles throbbing with pain. When Bates tried to knee Sutton in the groin, Sutton countered, thereby sending his opponent flying backward. Bates hit the floor with a resounding crash, causing the crowd that had gathered around the two men to *ooohhh* and *aaahhh.*

Bates sprang to his feet, a murderous gleam in his eyes, and thundered across the floor toward his target. Sutton met him head-on with a series of swift and well-placed body blows. He took several blows himself, one of them on the side of his head which caused him to lose sight of Bates for an instant. But he held on to consciousness and retaliated with a right uppercut, which he quickly followed up with a series of sharp jabs to the solar plexus.

Bates staggered backward, and then, recovering his balance, grabbed a chair and raised it high above his head in both hands.

Sutton leaped to one side as the chair came crashing down to the floor. He put out a foot and tripped Bates whose momentum had propelled him forward. As Bates went down, Sutton bent down, seized his opponent's coat collar, and hauled him to his feet. He marched the dazed man toward the door, intending to throw him out of the auditorium, but before he reached the door, Bates suddenly sprang to taut and angry life. He broke free of Sutton, spun around, and decked Sutton with a fast flurry of his hamlike fists.

Sutton's spine almost split as he hit the floor. Ignoring the pain the fall had caused him, he scrambled to his knees. But, before he could get to his feet, Bates' knee caught him under the chin. The blow threw him backward and again his spine blazed with pain as he hit the floor. He lay there stunned for a moment.

Then, as he saw Bates draw back a booted foot to kick him, he rolled out of the way of the oncoming blow and managed to get to his feet. He stood there, his fists clenched at his sides, as Bates lunged at him.

Sutton bent down and came in under Bates' upraised fists. When he straightened up again, he held the man above his head in both hands. He threw him and watched as Bates struck the wall and slid down it to lie in a crumpled heap on the floor. He waited a moment before turning and heading for the table where Miss

Parsons still sat, one hand clenched tightly against her chest.

He heard the shuffling movement behind him before he heard someone's shouted, "Look out!" He whirled around to find Bates up and coming at him.

A slug fest ensued with four fists flying, each one intent on doing as much damage as possible. Bates' nose broke under one of Sutton's particularly savage blows. Blood sprayed from it. When Sutton's other fist landed some seconds later on Bates' broken nose, it came away bloody.

Sutton, feeling a joyous kind of wildness surging within him, caught Bates off guard. He pounded the man as hard as he could with both fists—face, body, face again. Bates tried hard to fight him off. He did land one telling blow that almost downed Sutton, but the fight was going out of him. Sutton kept at the man, his fists hammering away, the wildness in him seeming to cancel out the pain in his hands and in other parts of his body.

Bates' fists began to droop. The blood oozing from his nose reddened his lips and chin. His eyes were glazed. But he was not finished. He brought his fists together, raised them high above his head, and before Sutton could block the blow, brought both of his fists down upon the top of Sutton's head.

Sutton fell to his knees, his head lolling forward as white lights blazed on a bright red ground in front of his eyes, which were stinging with the sweat that was running into them. Before Bates could hit him again, he lurched to one side and then staggered to his feet. He turned on Bates and ferociously attacked the man with punishing blows to the head, intent now on ending the fight by knocking Bates out.

He delivered a right hook, a left uppercut, several

sharp jabs, and then, as Bates was knocked backward by the attack, a devastating final punch. Bates' hands, no longer formed into fists, flew up into the air. He threw back his head as if he were about to shout but no words came from his lips. Slowly, he leaned away from Sutton and then rapidly fell face down on the floor, both arms flung out, his body motionless.

Sutton, panting, waited a moment, his eyes on Bates, but the man did not move. Sutton strode forward, bent down, got a grip on Bates' right wrist, and proceeded to drag him across the floor, out of the auditorium, down the hall, and finally out the front door of the school, where he left him lying in the dirt.

He was making his way back down the hall when a man he did not know came out of the auditorium and hurried up to him.

"Are you quite all right, Mr. Sutton?" the man asked him solicitously. "Shall I help you get to the doctor?"

"I'm fine."

"My name, Mr. Sutton, is William Smythe," the man announced. "I have, of course, read about you and your daring exploits in *The Territorial Enterprise,* which is what initially made me decide to seek you out. Now that I have seen how well you handle yourself, I am more than ever convinced that I have come to the right man."

"Come to the right man for what, Mr. Smythe, if you don't mind my asking?"

"I am a lawyer, Mr. Sutton. I recently represented a young man named Jimmy Lee Cranston. I have come to you for help in seeing to it that Jimmy Lee does not hang for a murder I am convinced he did not commit, but of which he has been found guilty in a court of law despite my best efforts to prove him innocent."

TWO

"I'm no lawyer, Mr. Smythe," Sutton said, "so I don't see how I can help you or your client."

"I know you're not a lawyer, Mr. Sutton," Smythe responded quickly. "I also know that you have a reputation—a well-deserved reputation from what I have read about you and your manhunts—as a tracker of missing persons."

Sutton said nothing.

Smythe continued, "This evening I was in despair over my failure to win Jimmy Lee Cranston's freedom. I had given up all hope of saving his life. But, as they say, it is always darkest just before the dawn. What I mean to say is I suddenly remembered what I had read about you in the newspaper and realized that you might very well be the man to help me save Jimmy Lee from the hangman's rope.

"Remembering from the newspaper accounts of your adventures, Mr. Sutton, that you were living at the International Hotel, when in town, I went there this evening only to find that you were out. I made inquiries of the desk clerk and he mentioned that you had told him you planned to attend the auction here at the school this evening. So I came here and was just in time to see your encounter with that brute who, it appeared to me, was trying to kill you." Smythe glanced apprehensively at the front door as if he feared the reappearance of Kernie Bates.

"I still don't see what it is you think I can do to save a man from a necktie party," Sutton said.

"Jimmy Lee is not really a man," Smythe said. "He is only sixteen. But to address your point, Mr. Sutton, let me tell you—have you not read about the trial in the newspaper?"

Sutton shook his head. As he did so, he suddenly recalled Miss Parsons telling Wright that she wished he wouldn't print stories about the murder that Jimmy Lee Cranston had been convicted of having committed.

"—there are three of them," he heard Smythe say and realized that he had not been paying attention to the man. "Beg pardon, Counselor. There are three of what?"

"Witnesses," Smythe replied. "A—uh, working woman, to put it charitably, named Etta Spode. Two men named Dennis Rutledge and Hank Tully. All three were present when Seth Grant was murdered at Miss Spode's business establishment. They all were, like Jimmy Lee himself, in the same room where and when the murder took place. Now, all three are gone. They have vanished, to coin a cliché, into thin air, Mr. Sutton. Don't you find that strange?"

"People pull up stakes and move on," Sutton commented noncommittally.

"If they had remained—made themselves available to testify at Jimmy Lee's trial—if even only one of them had done so—I am sure I could have proven Jimmy Lee innocent of the crime of murder. Surely, one or more of them must have seen something that night that would have exonerated my client. But they all disappeared the very night the murder was committed."

"Then who was there to point a finger at your client as the culprit?" Sutton inquired.

"There was a woman—one of Etta Spode's colleagues—who worked in the same parlor house. Her name is Janet Lowry. She had been entertaining a customer in another room of the house at the time of the murder. When she heard the shots, she and her customer—a man by the name of Wesley Hatfield—ran into the room where the killing took place—after taking some time to dress, of course—and found Jimmy Lee standing in the middle of the room with Seth Grant's gun in his hand. Grant was lying dead on the floor at Jimmy Lee's feet.

"Hatfield took Grant's gun from Jimmy Lee and Miss Lowry went for Sheriff Cobb. Both of them later testified at Jimmy Lee's trial that Jimmy Lee killed Seth Grant. I tried my best to point out that the evidence against the boy was circumstantial—to no avail."

"Where were the other three when this lady and her gentleman friend got to the scene of the crime?"

"They were all right there, according to Jimmy Lee. It was later, he said, just before Sheriff Cobb arrived on the scene that they disappeared."

"I take it you want me to find them for you."

"Yes, Mr. Sutton, I definitely do."

"You think one of the three killed Seth Grant?"

"I can't say that for sure. All I can say with certainty is that I find it very peculiar that the three disappeared before they could give their depositions to Sheriff Cobb. I hold in my heart the hope that one or more of them might be able to shed some additional light on what happened at Etta Spode's parlor house that night —some light which will prove my client innocent of the crime of which he has, in my opinion, been so unjustly convicted."

Smythe cleared his throat, shifted position, and said,

"Jimmy Lee will not be able to pay you for your services, I'm afraid. He is practically penniless. I was appointed by the court to defend him. I received my fee from the court fund set aside for the purpose of defending the indigent. But I am willing to pay you out of my own pocket, Mr. Sutton, if you will take on this task—and if your fee is not exorbitant."

"How about one hundred dollars a head, Counselor?"

"A fair fee, I should say," Smythe responded quickly. "Then you will try to find the three witnesses?"

"Glad to," Sutton said, eager to be in the saddle again and on his way, leaving Virginia City and its comforts and conveniences behind him for a time. You must be addled, he silently told himself. Anybody who'd give up a feather bed, the chance to take a hot bath now and then, and the fine food the International Hotel puts on its dining room tables in order to go traipsing all over hell's half-acre must be loco.

"Oh, I am ever so grateful to you, Mr. Sutton," Smythe cried, seizing and vigorously shaking Sutton's hand. "I know Jimmy Lee will be as well."

"I'll be wanting to have a talk with him before I set out," Sutton said.

"The sheriff's office is closed for the night but perhaps we could rouse Sheriff Cobb and ask him to open it so you could pay a visit to Jimmy Lee in his cell."

"Nope, let's don't do that. Sheriff Cobb and me have known each other for a long time, and I reckon we're friends—or at least not enemies. But were we to roust him out of his home like you're suggesting, I don't doubt for a minute he'd blame me for that rash act, and it wouldn't help our cause any, now would it? What say I go see Jimmy Lee first thing in the morning?"

"That would be fine, I suppose." Smythe lowered his gaze. "It's just that there is so little time left." He looked up at Sutton with mournful eyes. "Jimmy Lee is due to hang two weeks from today."

Sutton whistled through his teeth. "That sure doesn't give me a whole lot of time to track down three people. Now, Counselor, what can you tell me about the murder?"

"Well, as I said, it took place at the home of a woman named Etta Spode who lives on Sporting Row. Do you know that section of D Street, Mr. Sutton?"

"I've paid a visit or two in my time to some of the ladies who work there," Sutton answered.

"It seems there was a poker game taking place at Etta Spode's the night of the murder. It had apparently been organized by Seth Grant who is—who was—a professional, and some say a not very honest, gambling man. When Jimmy Lee arrived with the growler of beer that Etta Spode had sent to the saloon for—I should tell you that Jimmy Lee had been employed as a swamper in the saloon—the poker game was already in progress. Playing, in addition to Seth Grant, were the two men I mentioned—Dennis Rutledge and Hank Tully—the other two people who must have witnessed the murder and who, in addition to Etta Spode, I want you to find and bring back here. Well, Jimmy Lee arrived and—"

"Whoa," Sutton said, holding up a hand. "What can you tell me about the two men you just mentioned—Rutledge and Tully?"

"Dennis Rutledge is an ordinary and, as far as anyone knows, an upstanding citizen of the city. He has lived here for fourteen years and is the sole proprietor of the local feed and grain. He is married to a woman named Mary.

"Hank Tully is another matter altogether. He is a drifter and a gambler and, in stark and striking contrast to Rutledge, he does not enjoy an entirely savory reputation."

"Go on."

"Jimmy Lee arrived at Etta Spode's place of business with the growler of beer she had ordered, and he was soon enticed into joining the poker game by Seth Grant. He lost the little money he had to Grant. He claims that he caught Grant cheating, but Grant denied the charge and refused to give Jimmy Lee back the money he had lost during the time he was involved with the game."

So Jimmy Lee, Sutton thought, had himself a motive to kill Grant.

"This Jimmy Lee," he said, "has he got himself a temper?"

"I see what you're driving at, Mr. Sutton. I would be less than candid with you were I to deny that the boy definitely does have a temper. He admitted that he had argued with Grant about the money he had lost. But let me point out to you, Mr. Sutton, that Jimmy Lee was unarmed that night. In fact, he has never carried a gun —except on occasion a rifle to shoot squirrels with."

"What about Grant? I recall you saying, I think, that Jimmy Lee wound up with Grant dead, and Grant's gun was found in the boy's hand."

"That is correct. Mr. Grant was wearing a sidearm that night as was his habit, I understand. Let me add that Hank Tully was also armed that night. But not Mr. Rutledge."

"How about Miss Spode?"

"She has been known to carry a derringer tucked

under her garter but I don't know if she had one with her on the fatal night. She well might have."

"Your client—he claims he didn't see who shot and killed Grant even though he was in the room with those other three, any one of which could have done the deed?"

"I know that sounds hard to believe but that is his claim. I for one believe him."

"Well, I don't want—or really need—to dig too deep into the whys and wherefores of who killed Grant," Sutton said. "Convicting the real killer—assuming Jimmy Lee Cranston isn't the real killer—that's not my job. That's more in your line, Counselor. My job is just to bring back three people for you and the rest of the law's minions to go to work on."

"Precisely, Mr. Sutton. But I am willing to wager that once you have talked to Jimmy Lee tomorrow, you, like I, will be convinced of the boy's innocence."

"I got to say again, Counselor, who did Grant in is not my particular concern. The only reason I want to talk to your client is to find out what he can tell me about what he saw and heard happen the night Grant was murdered."

"If you will stop by my office tomorrow after visiting Jimmy Lee," Smythe said, "I will pay you your fee."

"I collect only if I can deliver the goods, Counselor," Sutton said. "The goods in this case being Etta Spode, Dennis Rutledge, and Hank Tully. But I will stop by your office if I have any more questions after I've talked with Jimmy Lee."

"My card," Smythe said, and handed an engraved business card to Sutton, who pocketed it and then made his way to the auditorium, his thoughts not on Jimmy Lee Cranston, but on Miss Letitia Parsons.

When Sutton awoke the following morning it was to greet the memory of the previous night and the time he had spent with Letitia Parsons. He lay on his bed, his eyes closed, seeing her face in his mind's eye. A faint smile curled his lips.

They had shared her box supper, and Sutton had thoroughly enjoyed it and Miss Parsons' sincerely expressed concern for him. Twice she had asked him if he was sure he was all right, and twice he had assured her that he was, although parts of his body were numb and other parts in pain.

Later, on the way to Miss Parsons' home, he was pleased at the way she took his arm. He couldn't recall what they had talked about but he knew they had talked. He did recall accepting her invitation to sit with her on her porch and the tart taste of the lemonade she brought him. The scent of honeysuckle that filled the night air was nowhere near as sweet for Sutton as was the perfume Miss Parsons wore. Sweet too was her nearness to him as they sat in the darkness of the mid-July night that was alive with the little lights of fireflies. Before they finally parted, he had asked her if he could come to call on her, and she had said he would be welcome.

He opened his eyes, and still smiling, sat up and swung his legs over the side of the bed. An hour later, after breakfasting in the hotel's dining room, he went whistling out of the building on his way to the sheriff's office.

When he reached it, he went inside and gave Sheriff Cobb, who was seated behind his battered desk, a nod and a cheerful, "Good day."

"Good day, indeed," responded Cobb grumpily.

"The alkali dust out there's thick enough to choke a horse."

"It almost always is, Sheriff. A man gets used to it."

"I never have and I never will," Cobb said and then coughed as if to prove his point. "What can I do for you, Luke?"

"You can let me have a word or two with one of your prisoners, Sheriff."

"I've only got one on my hands at the moment. Is it Jimmy Lee Cranston you want to talk to?"

"The same."

Sheriff Cobb's eyes narrowed as he got up and walked out from behind his desk. "What business have you got with him? The kid's as good as dead."

"But he's not dead yet. Now, Sheriff, are you going to make me give you my whole life's history before you let me in to see Jimmy Lee?"

"No need for you to get huffy about it," Cobb grumbled. "I was just wondering why you want to see a convicted killer, that's all. Are you fixing to get mixed up in my business again like you've done one or two times in the past as I recollect?"

"I don't get myself mixed up in your business, Sheriff. I mind my own."

Cobb's eyebrows rose in a gesture of exaggerated surprise. "Oh, do you, now? What about the way you got yourself mixed up in the murder of Dade McGrath not so long ago? That was my business, not yours."

"I didn't get mixed up in that matter until the town fathers saw fit to offer a bounty for the capture and return of Ted Kimball for doing in McGrath. A man has to earn his living, Sheriff."

"I'll grant you that much but I'll also remind you that you don't have to try taking my living away from me while you're earning yours. You made me look bad in that McGrath matter.''

"I didn't mean to, Sheriff, and that's the truth."

"Oh, I know it, Luke. Just don't pay any attention to me. I must have got up on the wrong side of the bed this morning. When a man gets to be my age he also tends to get cantankerous. How have you been keeping, Luke?''

"Tolerable, Sheriff, tolerable. Yourself?"

"Can't complain. Oh, I could. But nobody would listen. Come on in the back where I got the kid cooling his heels till the hangman shows up to claim him."

Sutton followed Cobb through a door to the cell area in the rear of the building. Cobb, using one of the keys on a ring he had taken from his desk in the outer office, opened a cell door and Sutton stepped inside the cell.

The boy he found there looked up from the bunk on which he was seated, and Sutton saw the fear in his eyes, the fear that was but a step or two away from terror. Two weeks from now, Sutton found himself thinking. In two weeks those eyes of his will be popping right out of his head with fright when they march him up the thirteen steps to the gallows.

"This here's a fellow named Luke Sutton, Jimmy Lee," Cobb said as he slammed and locked the cell door behind Sutton. "You give a holler, Luke, when you're ready to leave."

When Cobb had returned to the front office, Sutton said, "I'm not here to do you any harm, boy. I'm just here to talk."

"Talk? What about?"

Sutton leaned back against the bars and folded his arms across his chest. "You," he said, "and the murder of Seth Grant."

"I didn't kill him."

Sutton studied the boy who was seated so stiffly on the edge of the bunk. Jimmy Lee Cranston hadn't an extra ounce of flesh anywhere on his bones. He looks, Sutton thought, like a calf that can't find the feed lot. He had a plain face that spoke silently of sun and wind very much the way Sutton's did. His limbs were long and not through growing. His straight hair was so blond it was almost white. His guileless eyes were the blue of a jaybird. Sutton recalled Counselor Smythe telling him that Jimmy Lee was sixteen years old. He looks, Sutton thought, even younger than that. Fear's taken some years off him, turned him backward toward the time he was a child afraid of the dark.

"I should tell you right up front," Sutton said, "that it was your lawyer who got me to come here to have a talk with you."

"About—about the killing, you mean?"

It's the center of his world now, Sutton thought. He can't think of or see anything else excepting the murder of Seth Grant that they've gone and pinned on him. "That's right," he answered. "Counselor Smythe thinks I might be able to help you out of the fix you're in."

Jimmy Lee's eyes widened. Hope flared in them like a fanned fire. He half rose from his bunk—and then slumped back down upon it and lowered his head. "You can't do that. Nobody can. They're hell-bent on hanging me."

"They've not done so yet though. Where I come from there's a saying that goes 'Where there's life, there's hope.' "

Jimmy Lee continued sitting tensely on his bunk.

Sutton said to him, "I want you to make me a solemn promise."

Jimmy Lee gave him an uneasy look.

"I want you to promise me you'll ease up some. You look like a green bronc that's straining at a rope tied real tight to a snubbing post. I told you I didn't come here to harm you. So ease up now and stop looking like you think maybe I'm the man with the rope come to fetch you."

Jimmy Lee drew a deep breath and leaned back against the wall behind his bunk. He folded his hands in his lap and said, "It ain't been a bit easy to ease up when you've been run ragged like a rabbit with the hounds on his tail. Ever since that night when it happened, I feel like I been spun around and turned upside down until I don't know which way is up and which down or even what's real anymore."

"I'd like to talk about the night it happened," Sutton said.

"What do you want to know?"

"Tell me what happened once you got to Miss Spode's house."

"She had sent to the saloon where I worked—"

"For a growler of beer," Sutton interrupted. "I know that. Tell me what happened when you got to her house with the growler."

"She was the one let me in. She went to get the money to pay me, and while she was gone I stood around watching the men play cards—poker, it was. There was three of them. Mr. Rutledge, Mr. Tully and—and Mr. Grant."

Sutton noted the difficulty with which Jimmy Lee had spoken the last name, the name of the murdered Seth Grant. "Go on," he directed.

"Well, Mr. Grant, he seen me watching and he asked me did I want to sit in and play. I told him I didn't have but five dollars, and he said that didn't matter I should just come on and sit myself down and maybe, he said, I would walk away rich from that poker game. Well, sir, it sure was a tempting notion, so I took out my money and I sat myself down and I started in to play.

"Mr. Grant, he was real nice to me. So was Miss Spode when she come back and seen I was in the game. She stood behind me and she put one hand on my shoulder and she took to whispering words of encouragement to me every now and then."

Sutton suppressed a groan, remembering that Counselor Smythe had told him that Jimmy Lee had accused Seth Grant of cheating during the game. He could see the scene now. Etta Spode standing behind Jimmy Lee and somehow giving Grant signals about what cards the boy had in his hand. He said nothing, waiting for Jimmy Lee to go on.

"I started in to winning about then," Jimmy Lee continued. "I told Miss Spode I reckoned she had brung me some luck, and she got a laugh out of that. I won three times. By then I had close to twenty-five dollars on the table in front of me. But I started in to noticing that Mr. Grant kept looking over my head at Miss Spode and then quick away again. Well, I said to myself, why wouldn't he. Miss Spode's a well-turned-out woman that could easy catch any man's eye. But after awhile when I started in on a losing streak, I noticed that it was like as if Mr. Grant somehow knew exactly what cards I had in my hand. He beat me every time, along with Mr. Tully and Mr. Rutledge into the bargain.

"Then, it hit me right between the eyes. Miss Spode could see what cards I was holding, and somehow or other she was letting on to Mr. Grant what they was. I couldn't prove any of that though, not at the time. So I made up my mind to watch Mr. Grant real close, and it was but a few minutes later that I seen Mr. Grant was good at the false shuffle. I kept on watching close as a cat does a canary, and sure enough I seen Mr. Grant make a false cut—you know what that is, do you, Mr. Sutton?"

"I do. A false cut's when a dealer returns the halves of the deck to their original positions."

"Mr. Grant I seen was also slick at keeping a card on top of the deck till he needed it whilst he went merrily along dealing out the cards underneath. By that time my money was almost all gone. I knew that I had been played for a fool by Mr. Grant, and I wasn't about to let him get away with it. I work hard to earn my money, Mr. Sutton—and it's a thankless and dirty job I do for it too."

"Counselor Smythe told me you were a swamper in the saloon."

"It was about the best job I could land when I drifted into town. I quit school when I was in the third grade. I was never no scholar, Mr. Sutton, to tell you the plain truth. Book learning, it didn't and still don't come easy to me, and I used to feel bad that I kept getting left behind when other kids my age was moving on up to the next grade. It ain't that I'm dumb though. I can fix things and I can make most anything grow. My ma used to say when she was still among the quick that I could make turnips grow in solid sand."

Jimmy Lee grinned and so did Sutton.

"I hope to have me a farm of my own someday," the boy continued. "But till that day comes—" Jimmy Lee suddenly fell silent. Then, after a moment, "Anyway, what I did was accuse Mr. Grant of cheating me."

"What did he do when you did that?"

"He got mad. He said I was lying. He said I was just a sore loser is all. If I'd've won, he said, I wouldn't be calling him no cheater. Mr. Rutledge and Mr. Tully, they told me calm down, son, but I was past calming down I was that mad. Five dollars might not be much to men like them, but it was all I had for to feed and shelter myself with till payday come which was then four days down the road."

"Rutledge and Tully—they saw no sign that Grant had been false shuffling and dealing seconds?" Sutton asked.

Jimmy Lee met Sutton's steady gaze. "You think I didn't see what I say I seen, is that it?"

"Nope, it's not. I don't think that. I just asked a simple question and I'd be much obliged to you, boy, if you would answer it for me."

"They thought the game was on the up-and-up they said, only I knew for sure it weren't. I may not have much book learning, Mr. Sutton, but I got me a eye that's quick as a whip. I seen what I said I seen. Mr. Grant, he was cheating for sure. I even told him that I thought Miss Spode had been in on it with him. Of course, she said I was crazy as a loon for saying such a thing and so did he."

When Jimmy Lee fell silent again, obviously reliving in his memory the night of the murder, Sutton asked, "What happened then?"

"Mr. Rutledge says he thought it was time to call it quits. Mr. Tully, he got up and said he thought so too and then him and Mr. Rutledge, they gathered up their money and started for the front door. Miss Spode went with them to see them out."

"But you stood your ground?"

"I did. I got up and I told Mr. Grant I wanted him to

hand over the five dollars I had lost to him. He said I would get it over his dead body, and I said that wouldn't be so hard to arrange.

"It sure is funny, Mr. Sutton, the things a fellow will say that sometimes come back to haunt him. Like me telling Mr. Grant that maybe I would do him in if he didn't hand over my money."

"When did the shooting take place?"

"It was a few minutes later. Mr. Grant and me was facing each other across the table like two mules. I recollect I couldn't hear Miss Spode's voice no longer. She had been giggling and the like with Mr. Rutledge and Mr. Tully, but she weren't no longer, or if she was I couldn't hear her from wherever she was with the others that was behind me. I only heard a man's voice around that time.

"All of a sudden, a shot rang out like the last trump. Then another one come right on the heels of the first one. Then a third one—for good measure, I reckon. The first one, it caught Mr. Grant high up in the chest. He stood up like he was going to shoot back, but before he could get his gun out the second shot hit him in the cheek, and then the third one went into his chest same as the first one had.

"I tell you true, Mr. Sutton, I was so surprised I froze in my tracks. I couldn't take my eyes off of Mr. Grant and the blood that was all over him and the table and the money and the cards. He was like a sieve and that's a fact. I don't know how much time went by whilst I kept on staring at him, and he commenced to slide down to the floor while trying hard to stay up on his feet by holding tight to the table. He took it down with him when he went. Once he had hit the floor it was for me like a spell I'd been under had broken. I started in to thinking that whichever one of the three behind me who had shot Mr. Grant might decide to ventilate me too."

"The three shots—they came from behind you?"

Jimmy Lee scratched his head. "I think so though I couldn't swear to that. But I didn't see nobody else anywheres about."

"Go on."

"I started to turn around, wishing I had me a gun of my own in case somebody meant to shoot me too. I never made it. Somebody hit me from behind with something hard—maybe a gun butt, I'm not sure what it was—and down I went like Mr. Grant just had, with the only difference between the two of us being that he was dead and I was only knocked senseless."

"You didn't see who hit you?" Sutton inquired without much hope of a positive answer.

Jimmy Lee shook his head. "No, sir, I didn't. It could have been any one of the three of them. Anyway, when I come to I didn't know for a minute where I was. I was awful groggy, but then I got my wits about me and stood up. I was real shaky and I kept looking at the gun I had in my hand and wondering how it had got there. That's when Mr. Hatfield showed up on the stairs with Miss Lowry not long behind him. They're—"

"I know who they are. Where were they when the shooting took place?"

"Upstairs. I reckon they was in Miss Lowry's bedroom, though I couldn't swear on the Bible to that."

Sutton decided to have a talk with Lowry and Hatfield. Maybe one of them's the one who did in Grant, he thought.

"As Miss Lowry let out a scream," Jimmy Lee went on, "I turned around and seen Miss Spode and Mr. Rutledge and Mr. Tully. Miss Spode, she looked like she was scared to death of me. She put out a hand and said, 'Don't come near me!' and then, when Miss Lowry asked what happened down here, Miss Spode said, 'Jimmy Lee killed Seth with Seth's own gun!'

"Before I could say I didn't, Mr. Hatfield, he jumped me and took the gun off of me. 'Oh, thank God!' Miss Spode cried and then she told Miss Lowry to run and fetch the sheriff.

"Whilst we was all waiting for the sheriff to come, Mr. Hatfield held Mr. Grant's gun on me and told me if I made one wrong move he would stop my clock. I didn't make any kind of move at all, right or wrong, I was that scared. But I did a whole heap of fast thinking. I was trying to figure out how Mr. Grant's gun got in my hand, and the only thing I could come up with was that after whoever it was had knocked me out, somebody— maybe the same somebody who knocked me out—got Mr. Grant's gun and put it in my hand. But then I decided that didn't make no kind of sense a'tall.

"I mean who would want to do that to me? I was more or less a friend of Miss Spode's—or so I thought. I used to bring her a growler of beer most every night, and she had always treated me kindly. Mr. Rutledge and Mr. Tully—those two I never ever had had a hard word with. I had never even laid eyes on Mr. Hatfield before that night. As for Miss Lowry, she never give me so much as the time of day, so I couldn't see her having any kind of grudge against me."

Sutton found himself marveling at the fact that there was still innocence abroad in the world as personified in this instance by Jimmy Lee and the boy's view of the five people at the scene of the murder. He really doesn't realize, he thought, that any one of those five people could have put Grant's gun in his hand for no other reason than to protect themselves—or one of their number. The boy, he thought, could have been born yesterday considering the guileless way he thinks.

He said, "You told me before, boy, that you drifted into Virginia City. Where did you drift from?"

"Tinkersville," Jimmy Lee answered. "I had me a job in a livery barn there. Tinkersville is due east of here. It's just a jerkwater town. I left there to come here and see the big city."

"Were you born and raised in Tinkersville?"

"No. I was born and raised up on a farm in Missouri. My ma died when I was eleven. After she went, Pa took to the bottle with a vengeance. He was a good man when he was sober. But drunk he was hell with the lid off. He took to abusing me when he had drunk too much. It wasn't that he was a mean man or anything like that. It was, I always reckoned, that Ma dying the swift way she did and so young had hurt him real bad, and he needed to hurt somebody back to try to get even. I know that don't sound altogether sensible but that's how it seemed to me at the time. But I finally gave up on Pa. Had to, else I would have wound up with maybe some broken bones or worse. So one night I made up my mind and that same night I left the homeplace. I never went back. I went from here to there, always looking for the land of my dreams but never finding it. I had me five years of fiddlefooting my way from Missouri to here. Now it looks like I've come to the end of the line, don't it?"

"Maybe. Maybe not."

"What's that supposed to mean?"

"That's supposed to mean that I am going to try to find Etta Spode, Dennis Rutledge, and Hank Tully and if I do find them I mean to bring them all back here so maybe they can tell the sheriff what really happened that night and get you off the hook you're on. It also means that I am going to look up Janet Lowry and Wesley Hatfield and have a talk with them about what happened."

"What for are you going to do all that?"

Sutton thought of the hundred dollars a head Counselor Smythe had agreed to pay him if he brought back the three people who were present when Grant was murdered. But that money, he knew, wasn't the reason —at least, not the only reason—he was going man- and, in this particular case, woman-hunting again. He was doing it, he realized with some surprise, because now that he had met and listened to Jimmy Lee Cranston, he wanted to see to it that the boy had a chance to get on with trying to find the land of his dreams.

"I'm doing it," he told Jimmy Lee, "to keep that rope they've got ready and waiting from slipping down around your neck, that's why."

"Then you believe I didn't do it?"

"I believe you didn't do it."

Jimmy Lee let out a sibilant sigh and then, "I can't pay you for your time and trouble, Mr. Sutton," he said in a voice that was at once despairing and hopeful.

"Your lawyer's doing that."

Jimmy Lee rose and held out his hand. "I'm mighty grateful to you, Mr. Sutton."

As Sutton shook hands with the boy, Jimmy Lee lost control. A sob burst from between his lips. He turned away from Sutton, his shoulders shaking. After awhile he regained control of himself and said, but without turning around to face Sutton, "I'm sorry. It's just that I've been so bad scared. So scared and so all alone. Now here you come all set to lend me a helping hand out of this mess I've gone and got myself in and well, it just got to me is all."

"Boy, I mean to do my best to see you don't hang. I can't promise you that that won't happen." Sutton saw Jimmy Lee's body stiffen. "But I can promise you that I'll do my damndest to see that it doesn't. Be seeing you."

THREE

Sutton was on his way out of the office after Sheriff Cobb had let him out of Jimmy Lee's cell when Cobb stopped him by saying, "I overheard some of what you were saying to the kid, Luke."

Sutton, at the door, turned around. "Why, I never figured you for a listener at keyholes, Sheriff."

"I wasn't listening at any keyhole. The door was wide open and you've got a voice that tends to carry. I bring this up because I want to tell you straight out and up front that I don't want you interfering in this matter."

"What matter's that?" Sutton asked although he knew very well what Cobb was referring to.

"The matter of the People versus Jimmy Lee Cranston," Cobb declared. "It's cut and dried. It's over and done with."

"You're wrong on that last point, Sheriff," Sutton remarked mildly. "It won't be over and done with till Jimmy Lee is either hanged or let loose."

"Now, there you go again, Luke," Cobb muttered, shaking his head, clearly annoyed. "From what I heard you say just now you're fixing to try to turn things around, muck things up, make a general nuisance of yourself. I'm here to tell you the investigation of the Grant killing was handled in the right way."

"I've not the slightest doubt you did your best, Sheriff. But your best didn't help Jimmy Lee a whole lot or so it appears to me."

"I tell you I felt bad about how that trial came out, Luke, and that's the truth. The kid didn't have the chance of a snowflake in hell. But that doesn't change the way I feel about you planning to go out after those three missing persons. That's going to make me look bad. It will make people think I didn't do my job right. I want to get elected to another term, Luke, and if you find Spode and the other two and bring them back here and then they give the kid a new trial and he's found not guilty for one reason or another—it will look like you did what I should have done for him in the first place— find the witnesses which, I tell you, I tried my very best to do. But I couldn't turn up a trace of any one of them. I had this office to run—people didn't stop committing crimes. I was kept busier than a one-armed man in a fistfight. If I had had deputies—if I had had even *one* deputy—then things might have been different. I could have assigned a deputy to try to track down Spode and the two men. But I *didn't* have a deputy."

Sutton began to smile.

"What's tickling you?" Cobb asked gruffly.

"How about if you deputize me, Sheriff? How about if you send me out as your right-hand lawman—armed with subpoenas for those three witnesses? Wouldn't that make you look good—if I can find them and bring them back here?"

"Sure, it would make me—and you too—look good," Cobb agreed.

"Is it a deal then, Sheriff?"

"It's a deal." Cobb sat down at his desk and quickly wrote out three subpoenas—one for Etta Spode, one for Dennis Rutledge, and one for Hank Tully—which he handed to Sutton. Then he rummaged through a desk drawer until he found what he was looking for—a tin

star with the words Virginia City Deputy Sheriff engraved on it. He pinned the star to Sutton's lapel.
"There you go. That makes it official."

"Don't I get sworn in or something?"

Cobb waved away the question. "I think we can dis-
pense with the formalities, don't you?"

"Be seeing you, Sheriff," Sutton said and reached for
the doorknob.

"One last thing before you go, Luke."

Sutton waited expectantly.

"I wish you luck, Luke. I hope you can do something
for Jimmy Lee. The kid got a bad deal, there's no two
ways about that."

Sutton rubbed his coat sleeve over his deputy's badge
to polish it and then left the office.

He returned to the International Hotel and when he
left it an hour later he was wearing a blue cotton shirt,
leather vest, faded jeans tucked into his army boots, a
checkered bandanna around his neck, and a black
slouch hat. Around his lean hips was strapped a leather
cartridge belt, none of its loops empty. In the holster
that hung from the belt was a six-shot Remington Im-
proved Army Revolver, Model 1875, caliber .45. It was
made of plain blue steel and had equally plain walnut
grips. He had removed the lanyard ring from it so that
the gun would draw easily, and it was for that same
reason that he had lightly oiled the inside of the holster
that housed the weapon.

He took the business card Counselor Smythe had
given him from his pocket. Noting the address printed
on the card, he started down C Street. He had passed
the red brick and iron-faced building that was the home
of *The Territorial Enterprise* when he heard his name

called. He turned to find William Wright standing in the street and beckoning to him. He retraced his steps.

"I saw you passing by, Luke," Wright began when Sutton reached him, and then he exclaimed, "Hello, what's this?" He pointed to the tin star pinned to Sutton's vest.

"I'm a brand new deputy sheriff, Bill," Sutton answered, and then told Wright how and why he had become one.

"Then I was right," the newspaper editor exclaimed. "When I saw through the window that you were not wearing town clothes, I suspected you were leaving the city and assumed that there might be a story lurking behind that seemingly prosaic fact and so there is as it turns out, so there is."

"I wish you wouldn't keep on writing so lurid about me in that newspaper of yours, Bill. I'm getting to be about as notorious as Wes Hardin, thanks to all the gaudy things you write about me."

"I'll stop writing about you, Luke, when you stop making the gaudy—to use your own word against you—news my subscribers love to read about. How's that for a bargain?"

Sutton grinned as Wright gave him a wink. "You've got me there, Bill. I reckon I'll not stop my now-and-then manhunting so it seems clear you won't stop writing stories about me."

"And this one sounds like a real winner to me," Wright exclaimed enthusiastically. "Local lawman hunts murder witnesses to save convicted killer from rope," he intoned solemnly. "I'll get right on it, Luke. Good luck to you—and be careful!"

Sutton turned and continued making his way to the office of Counselor Smythe. When he reached it, he gave his name to the law clerk seated at a desk and told the man he wanted to see Smythe. The clerk left the room and returned a moment later to usher Sutton into an adjoining office, where Smythe rose from behind a desk and shook hands with Sutton.

"I need some information from you, Counselor," Sutton said. "Namely, the addresses of Etta Spode, Dennis Rutledge, and Hank Tully."

Smythe wrote three addresses on a piece of paper, which he handed to Sutton. "Spode and Rutledge had permanent addresses here in town which I've given you but the one for Tully—it's a boarding house. He was there no more than two days preceding the murder."

Sutton pocketed the paper. "Be seeing you, Counselor."

"Godspeed, Mr. Sutton."

Sutton went first to the address he had been given for the Spode place of business, which was on the stretch of D Street known to Virginia City residents as Sporting Row. A young woman Sutton estimated to be no more than twenty years old responded to his knock by opening the door and giving a low moan when she saw the star pinned to his vest.

"I'm not here to give you any trouble, miss," he hastily assured her.

She gave him a sly smile. "Then what are you here to give me?"

"I'm looking to have a talk with a woman named Janet Lowry who I was told lives here."

"Well, honey, you've found her. Now what?" Another smile, as sly as the first.

"I wonder could I step inside and have a few words with you, Miss Lowry."

She hesitated and then stepped aside, allowing Sutton to enter the house. After she had closed the door, she led him to a parlor on one side of the house and pointed to a chair. He waited until she had seated herself, and then he sat down in the chair she had indicated.

"I understand," he began, "you were here the night Seth Grant was murdered, Miss Lowry."

"Hey, wait a minute, mister!" she cried. "I thought that business was all over and done with. They're fixing to hang Jimmy Lee Cranston for that crime. So what are you doing nosing around here like that Sheriff Cobb was doing for so long I almost had to take him in as a boarder?"

"I'd be obliged to you if you'd tell me what you saw and heard that night," Sutton said without answering her question.

She slumped down in her chair. "I was upstairs when it happened," she began in a lifeless monotone. "I heard three shots. I knew they were shots because in my line of work you get to hear a lot of shots and after awhile there's no mistaking them for, say, firecrackers. I was with a customer, a Mr. Hatfield. He wanted to go downstairs and see what was going on but I told him if he did he might get shot. Let's just stay here and, you know, I told him.

"But he got ever so fidgety. I tried to calm him down but I couldn't. Anyway, when I saw it was no use trying to give him what he had come to me for, I said, 'All right, if you want to go down and maybe get your head blown off, don't let me stop you, go right ahead.' So he got dressed and down he went."

"Did you hear anything after the three shots?"

"Not a thing. Well, I waited a few minutes and then

my curiosity got the best of me. I pulled on my wrapper and crept to the top of the stairs. I could see Mr. Hatfield standing halfway down the steps. He was staring at something I couldn't see. I went down one step and then two more but I still couldn't see anything. I heard people talking though. I recognized my friend's voice—Etta Spode's voice. I also heard men's voices but I didn't know whose voices they were.

"I was almost down to where Mr. Hatfield was standing when I got to thinking about curiosity killing the cat. I was ready to run back to my room when I thought, in for a penny, in for a pound. So down I went, and when I saw Seth Grant lying on the floor with blood all over him, I screamed. Jimmy Lee Cranston was standing there with a gun in his hand. He turned around and made like he was heading for Etta and she told him, 'don't you come near me.' I asked Etta what had happened and she said Jimmy Lee shot Mr. Grant to death with Mr. Grant's own gun because the kid claimed Seth was cheating him at cards.

"I told Mr. Hatfield to do something. So he sneaked down the stairs while Jimmy Lee had his back turned, and he jumped the kid. He got the gun away from Jimmy Lee and held it on him. That's when Etta sent me for the sheriff. When Sheriff Cobb got here, Etta, Hank, and Dennis Rutledge were all gone. Sheriff Cobb asked me and Mr. Hatfield about what had happened. We told him."

"What?" Sutton prompted.

"That Etta had said that Jimmy Lee claimed Mr. Grant had cheated him at cards, and when Mr. Grant wouldn't give him back the money he had lost, Jimmy Lee grabbed Mr. Grant's gun and shot him three times with it. Those were the shots I heard when I was still upstairs."

"What did Jimmy Lee have to say for himself?"

"Oh, my, you should have heard the wild and totally unbelievable story he told to the sheriff. He said somebody hit him from behind and knocked him out. He said it was while he was out cold that Mr. Grant got shot. But the sheriff, as you might well imagine, didn't believe a word he said. So Sheriff Cobb took him into custody, and Jimmy Lee was tried fair and square and he's set to hang in two weeks."

Sutton considered what he had just heard before asking, "Do you think it's at all possible that one of the three people in the room with Grant that night besides Jimmy Lee could have killed Grant?"

"Not Etta," Janet responded sharply. "Etta would never kill the goose that was laying golden eggs for her."

"Mr. Grant, I take it from what you say, was good to Miss Spode?"

"Good as gold." Janet tittered behind one hand. "He gave her gifts galore. No, Etta was nobody's dummy. She certainly wouldn't have cut off her nose to spite her face by killing Mr. Grant even if she hated him, which I am here to tell you she definitely didn't. She told me that he was the best man she had had in a coon's age."

"What about Rutledge and Tully? Could either of them have done it, in your opinion?"

Janet placed the tip of an index finger on her chin and pondered Sutton's question. "I don't think so."

"Why not?"

"For one thing, Hank Tully had never even met Seth Grant until that night. For another, Mr. Rutledge isn't the killing kind."

"How do you know Tully had never met Grant before that night?"

"Because I was there earlier in the evening when he arrived and Etta introduced him to Mr. Grant."

"How do you know that Rutledge is not what you call 'the killing kind,' Miss Lowry?"

"He's as meek as a mouse, that's why. Etta told me that he had come here that one time—the night Mr. Grant was murdered—because his wife was eight months pregnant and he didn't want to touch her for fear he would hurt her. It was an accident pure and simple that he happened to be here that awful night. But that nasty Jimmy Lee—that's another matter altogether."

"What do you mean by that?"

"He lost money to Mr. Grant that night. He accused Mr. Grant of cheating him at cards. *He's* the only one who had a reason to kill Mr. Grant, and I for one have no doubt that he did."

"Do you have any idea where Miss Spode might have gone that night?"

"No. She was all alone in the world. She had no kin that I ever knew of. But there are lots of places for a girl like her to go if she wants to keep on working."

"What about the two men who disappeared? Do you have any idea where they might be?"

Janet's eyes widened. "I get it. You're going to try to find them! That's it, isn't it?"

"Yes, it is."

"Well, then, I'm not going to say another word to you. If you should find Etta and bring her back here, that Jimmy Lee Cranston might bust out of jail and wring her neck until she is dead. I won't let that happen to my dearest friend in all the world. Get out of here, Mr. Lawman!"

Sutton, bemused, rose and headed for the door.

His next stop was at the home of Dennis Rutledge, or what had been Rutledge's home before his sudden disappearance. When an obviously pregnant woman opened the door in response to his knock, he asked, "Are you Mrs. Rutledge?"

"Yes, I am," the woman replied, her eyes fixed on Sutton's star. "I'm Mary Rutledge. You're—" She looked up at Sutton.

"Namc's Luke Sutton, ma'am."

"You're a lawman, I see by your badge."

"At the moment I am, yes. I've come here to have a talk with you about your husband."

"About Dennis? What can I tell you that I have not already told Sheriff Cobb?"

"Maybe nothing. Maybe something. Would you mind if I came inside out of the sun, Mrs. Rutledge? It does bear down hot and hard this time of year."

"Come in then if you must."

Sutton followed Mrs. Rutledge into the house, and when they were seated in the front room, he said, "You have a real nice place here. It's a wonder to me that your husband would want to up and leave it the sudden way he did."

Mrs. Rutledge looked away from Sutton. The fingers of her right hand beat a silent tattoo on the overstuffed arm of the chair in which she was sitting so stiffly, her back rigid, her shoulders squared.

When she said nothing, Sutton said, "I guess he just didn't fancy being mixed up in the middle of a murder."

Mrs. Rutledge turned her head and stared at Sutton.

"Why are you here now? The killer of Mr. Grant has been tried and convicted. Why is the law still interested in my husband?"

"I'm here," Sutton said, "to find out where you think he might be, Mrs. Rutledge. I want to find that out so I can go wherever it is he's at and bring him back here and have him tell his tale about what happened that night to Sheriff Cobb."

"But Dennis could only tell you that he saw Jimmy Lee Cranston kill Mr. Grant in cold blood."

"I'm not so sure it happened that way, Mrs. Rutledge."

"Dennis wouldn't lie," she said hotly, her face flushing. "The other two—well, I can't speak for the likes of a fancy woman and a drifter. But I know my Dennis. He is not a liar. He is a decent man and an upstanding citizen of this city."

Sutton hesitated a moment and then, reluctantly, said, "Some folks there are who would say that any man who spends time in a house run by the likes of Miss Etta Spode doesn't quite qualify as 'decent.' "

Mrs. Rutledge recoiled in her chair as if Sutton had just threatened her with bodily harm.

"I'm not one of those folks," he quickly added but he knew the damage had been done just as he knew he had had to do it. "Did you know he was at Miss Spode's that night, Mrs. Rutledge?"

She shook her head and then lowered her gaze to her hands, which were twisting nervously in her lap. "That's the reason Dennis disappeared," she murmured.

"Beg pardon, ma'am?" Sutton said, not sure he had heard her correctly.

She looked up at him, her face pale now, her voice

low, and said, "He couldn't stand to face me after that night. He was undoubtedly ashamed of himself for having gone to that—that place and that woman. So he went away."

"I was told that the three witnesses to the murder disappeared the night it happened. So your husband never did come back to you that night or the next day. Is that so?"

"Yes. Oh, I would have forgiven Dennis. I wish he had come back to me. I would have tried to make him love me again. Oh, Mr. Sutton, I would have tried so *hard!*"

Sutton knew the tears would come and come they did. Mrs. Rutledge hid her face in her hands and wept quietly for several minutes.

When her tears ended and she had taken her hands away from her face, Sutton said, "Janet Lowry, who is a friend of Miss Spode's, told me your husband had never been to their house before. She said he told her that he had come only because you were pregnant and he didn't want to risk hurting you. I don't mean to embarrass you, ma'am, nor do I want to speak out of turn. I just wanted to tell you that in the hope that it will ease your hurting some and so you won't think too bad of your husband."

"I don't understand," Mrs. Rutledge whispered, her eyes fastened on Sutton's face.

"What is it you don't understand?"

"I recognized your name when you told it to me at the door. I remember reading about you in the *Enterprise.* I have heard stories whispered about you—your brutality, your gunslinging ways, and your callous disregard for the lives of the men you've killed."

Sutton, taken by surprise by what Mrs. Rutledge had

just said, was about to protest but she prevented him from doing so by continuing, "I now believe, after just witnessing your kindness toward me, which is definitely not the act of a brutish man, that those stories I have heard and read must surely have been distorted."

"I've never laid claim to sainthood," Sutton said, "but neither am I the kind of man you heard about in those stories you mentioned, I can assure you."

"Mr. Sutton, I take it that you don't believe Jimmy Lee Cranston committed the murder."

"I do tend to believe him when he says he didn't do it, yes. His story made sense to me about how somebody slugged him from behind, and when he came to Seth Grant's gun was in his hand and its owner was dead." Sutton paused a moment and then said, "Mrs. Rutledge, let me ask you this. Where do you think your husband might be at the moment?"

"I don't know although I have given that question much thought. It's possible he might have gone back East to where his mother resides in Philadelphia. But I can't really believe he has deserted me for good. Sometimes I think I see him on the street. But when I hurry to catch up with the man who looked a little like him, it turns out to have been a trick of the light or the play of shadow and it is not my Dennis. Oh, I do miss him so. I want to believe—I have to believe—that he will come back to me. To me and—our baby."

As Mrs. Rutledge's hands came to rest on her swollen belly, Sutton said, "If your husband didn't go far, where do you think he might go that's near?"

"Well, I don't think he would stay here in town. He would be sure to be seen and recognized."

"I was told he ran the feed and grain in town. Was that the only kind of work he ever did?"

"No. Before we were married, Dennis moved around quite a bit. He did all sorts of things. He was a cook, a day laborer, and for a time he ran a freighting business between Virginia City and Sacramento with a friend of his. His former partner still runs the business and used to like to tease Dennis about having given up his foot-loose life for one of placid domesticity." Mrs. Rutledge managed a fond, but rather wan, smile.

"What was his partner's name?"

"Paul Morrison."

"Where did your husband last work as a cook?"

"Right here in town—at the Tiptoe Inn."

"And before that?"

"At a restaurant in Dodge City. I can't recall the name of the place at the moment. Is it important?"

Instead of answering the question, Sutton asked, "Do you have a picture of your husband I could take a gander at?"

Mrs. Rutledge rose and went to a table on the far side of the room. She returned carrying a framed photograph which she handed to Sutton.

He studied the wedding picture she had given him. Dennis Rutledge stood to one side of his seated bride, his right hand resting on her shoulder as he stared solemnly at the camera. He was a sturdily built man with a blocky body and a square face. He wore a mustache and a goatee that gave him a faintly saturnine look which was largely offset by his mirthful eyes.

"What color are his eyes and hair, Mrs. Rutledge?" Sutton asked.

"His hair and eyes are both brown."

Sutton returned the photograph and got to his feet.

"Do you think you will be able to locate Dennis?"

Mrs. Rutledge asked him as she rose and walked with him to the front door.

"I don't know, to be blunt about it," he replied. "But I sure am going to try to find him."

"If you do locate Dennis, Mr. Sutton, please tell him to come home to me. Tell him I miss him terribly and that I need him desperately. With the baby coming, I—"

Seeing that Mrs. Rutledge was unable to continue, Sutton said, "I'll tell him," and then he left the house.

FOUR

Sutton paid a visit to the boarding house where Hank Tully had stayed, and was told by the woman who ran the establishment that she could give him no information about Tully except to say that he had never returned to his room on the night of Grant's murder. As far as she was concerned, she said, she hoped she had seen the last of him, since boarders involved with murder, innocent though they may be, would give her house a bad name.

Sutton's next stop was at the freight office of the railroad depot. There he introduced himself to the freight clerk and asked him if Paul Morrison still made freight runs between Virginia City and Sacramento.

"Sure, he does," the clerk answered. "Paul Morrison will be a teamster till the day he dies."

"Does he come to town regular?"

"About once a month on average, I'd say."

"When was he last here?"

"Let's see, that would be—last week, it was—a Tuesday, I think. He brought some bolts of Chinese silk which made all the ladies in town pretty happy and some ginger and some tools for use in the mines."

"Did he seem the same as usual to you when he was here last week?"

"He did."

"Did he say anything unusual?"

The freight clerk considered the question a moment and then shook his head. "No, Morrison didn't say anything unusual that I can recall. But he did something unusual."

"Oh? What did he do that struck you as unusual?"

"Well, Morrison, when he comes to town, never fails to help me unload the wagons. He knows I got the rheumatism bad in my back so he helps me unload. Morrison's a big man and a strong one too. With his help the work goes fast. Only this time he left me to do the unloading all on my own. I didn't complain, you understand. After all, it is my job."

"Where'd he go, the saloon?"

"Maybe he did. I've got no way of knowing that. But one place he did go was the dry goods store. I know that for sure because he had some parcels with him when he came back here. I recognized the paper they were wrapped in. Only Ed Munch who owns the dry goods store uses pink paper to wrap his parcels in. I guess the ladies like it. Mister, how come you're asking me all these questions?"

"I'm trying to find out who killed Seth Grant."

"You're trying to find out who—here you are wearing a lawman's badge and you don't know Jimmy Lee Cranston killed Grant?"

"Bear with me, will you? I understand that Dennis Rutledge used to be partners with Paul Morrison in the freighting business."

"They were, that's true enough. But what in the world has them being partners got to do with Grant's murder?"

"Nothing maybe. By the way, where does Morrison have his headquarters? Here or in Sacramento?"

"Neither place. He has himself a place in the Sierras about fifty miles from here on the stage road."

"I'm obliged to you," Sutton said, about to leave.

But before he could do so, the freight clerk said, "You're wasting your time, Deputy."

"I am?"

"Sure you are. You said before you wanted to find out who killed Seth Grant. Well, like I said before, everybody knows who did that dastardly deed. It was Jimmy Lee Cranston and you must know he's sitting in jail right this very minute waiting for a visit from the hangman."

Sutton didn't argue with the man.

From the freight office, he went directly to the Tiptoe Inn where he asked to see the man who ran it. He was taken to the kitchen by a white-aproned young woman who pointed to a man in shirtsleeves who was working frantically at a large iron stove on which several pots steamed and boiled. "That's Mr. Everett," the waitress said. "He owns this place."

Sutton thanked the waitress and went over to Everett. "I wonder could I ask you some questions about a man named Dennis Rutledge."

"No, you can't," said the man as he stirred the contents of one pot while simultaneously sprinkling salt in another one. "I'm busy. Even if I weren't I wouldn't talk to you about Rutledge. The man's a bounder."

Sutton's interest was aroused. "What makes you say that?"

"I say it because it's true," Everett muttered, sweat from his face and huge forearms falling into a frying pan full of sizzling steaks. "Angela!" he roared.

The young waitress appeared in the kitchen doorway a moment later.

"Here," Everett said to her, forking steaks onto two plates and smothering them in fried onions. "Don't keep your customers waiting."

"Yes, sir," Angela said and fled with the two plates.

"Can't get decent help these days," Everett complained. "The girl's a dawdler. Rutledge was a bull-headed so-and-so."

"What do you mean?"

"I tried to give him the benefit of my advice about how to cook properly. But would he take it? He would not. He told me I had hired him as the cook and he would cook things his way or be damned. I can't tell you how many fights we had in this kitchen. The man simply would not listen to reason. He was a good cook. I was trying to help him learn to be a great one. This restaurant is my business after all. He was ruining it."

"The customers complained, did they, about Rutledge's cooking?"

"No, but he wasn't giving them the best that he could have given them. I mean if he had been willing to do things my way. Well, the long and the short of it is he wouldn't. I told him he would either do things my way or he wouldn't do them at all—not here, not in my place. Well, one thing led to another and I finally fired him. It's a wonder I didn't kill him, he made me that mad. *Angela!*"

The waitress returned on the run and Everett thrust three plates of food at her which she took from him and hurriedly left.

"Get out of here, Deputy," Everett ordered Sutton. "I have no time to talk to you now. I already told you that. Especially not about Rutledge who practically put me out of business the way he seemed hell-bent on poisoning my customers."

Sutton left the kitchen. As he was making his way out of the restaurant, Angela stopped him. With a nervous glance at the kitchen door, she whispered, "Don't listen to Mr. Everett. He can't keep good help. Especially cooks. He wants to do everything his way and cooks can be the most cantankerous of men. He runs the kitchen himself these days because no cook will work for him."

"Angela!" Everett bellowed from the kitchen and the waitress abandoned Sutton.

Once outside, he headed for the livery barn, where he kept his horse when he was in town. He thought as he walked of what little he had learned from the people he had spoken to so far. Etta Spode, he thought, could be working in any parlor house within a hundred miles of here. I wouldn't mind looking for her in them but it does seem like a scattergun kind of approach to start with.

As far as Hank Tully is concerned, I've got even less to go on. A drifter with no roots and no ties to anywhere that I know of. Going after him would be like hunting a whisper in a big wind. Which leaves me with Rutledge and only one thing where he's concerned strikes me as sure, and that's that he wouldn't be likely to go to his former employer, Mr. Everett, for help or a hiding place. That would be like putting two strange bulldogs in a cage together and letting them tear each other to pieces.

Which leaves me the choice of looking up Paul Morrison to see if he's heard from his former partner or going up to Dodge City to find the restaurant Rutledge worked in up there to see if that's where he went. Or going to Philadelphia where his mother's at. Which I don't relish doing neither. Not at this point, at any rate.

Minutes later, as Sutton was passing the dry goods store, he halted and thought for a moment. He wondered if anyone inside the store could tell him anything of interest about Paul Morrison. He doubted it. But, hell, he thought. Drowning men catch at straws, don't they? And with the little bit of information I've been able to turn up so far on the three people I'm out to find, I'm starting to see the water rising round my boots.

A moon-faced man behind the counter rubbed his hands together at the sight of Sutton entering his store and gave out with a somewhat shrill, "May I be of some service, sir?"

"Are you by any chance Ed Munch?" Sutton inquired.

"Yes, sir, I am the sole proprietor of this emporium. What may I do for you, sir?"

"The freight clerk down at the depot told me a man by the name of Paul Morrison was in your place last week—on a Tuesday, he thinks."

"Ah, yes, Mr. Morrison, the teamster. He purchased a pair of boots, size eight and one half; two flannel shirts, medium; men's stockings and undergarments; a pair of trousers, thirty-two waist, twenty-nine inseam." Munch paused, studying Sutton. "What is the nature of your interest in Mr. Morrison, Deputy, if I may be so bold as to ask?"

"I'm trying to track down a man, and that man and Morrison used to be in business together."

"You must be referring to Mr. Dennis Rutledge."

"That's the man."

"Mr. Rutledge, I've heard, has disappeared."

"You heard right. I'm trying to track him down on behalf of his wife," Sutton lied.

"Well, I don't know what I can tell you that would help you except that Mr. Morrison has been a regular customer of mine for a number of years but what good that will do you I can't imagine."

"Morrison buys a lot of clothes here, does he?"

"No, he doesn't."

"But you just said he bought—"

"That large order of clothes was the exception rather than the rule," Munch stated. "Generally, Mr. Morrison buys his clothes in California although he once did buy a hat here. His was blown off by one of our famous—or should I say infamous—zephyrs, as we call the winds here in town. It was hopelessly mangled by a passing mule train. Usually Mr. Morrison buys only rock candy here. He has quite a sweet tooth, has Mr. Morrison."

Munch thoughtfully massaged his chin. "It was odd. I thought so at the time and I still think so."

"Odd? What was?"

"The clothes Mr. Morrison bought. He told me they were for himself. Made a point of saying so. But the clothes he selected were much too small for him, as I pointed out at the time. You see, Mr. Morrison is a big man but the sizes he chose were for a much smaller man. I asked him to try them on to prove my point but he wouldn't. I warned him that all sales in this particular emporium are final. Still, he bought them while still insisting they were for himself. Now, don't you think that's odd?"

"I'm obliged to you, Mr. Munch, for the information."

"Sir"—Munch called out as Sutton headed for the door—"we have a special this week on gent's outerwear of all kinds. May I show you—"

But Sutton was gone.

Later that day, after he had eaten and retrieved his dun from the livery barn, Sutton rode west out of town, still mulling over what Munch had told him about Morrison.

Morrison says he's buying clothes for himself, he thought, and then he goes and buys sizes too small for him—according to Munch who ought to know. Those clothes he bought may turn out to have been for somebody else, maybe somebody who couldn't show his face in town to buy them for himself. And that somebody else just might turn out to be Dennis Rutledge.

It's something worth looking into, he thought. Especially so when I've got no other strong lead of any kind to any of the other two missing persons. Besides, even if I'm wrong about who Morrison bought the clothes for, it behooves me to pay a visit to the man, just in case he can give me some kind of line on where Rutledge might have gone to ground if he's not at his former partner's place.

He rode on, his hands resting lightly on his saddle horn, the dun under him blinking into the sun up ahead that was drifting down toward the still snow-capped peaks of the Sierra Nevada mountains, turning them from a blinding white to a mellow gold and then, as the minutes passed, to a deep mauve before they were almost lost to view when the sun slid down behind them.

Before the last of the day's light had faded, Sutton, his belly growling, found a sheltered copse in the foothills, where he dismounted and began to gather wood. Minutes later, he had a good fire burning under some quaking aspens, its smoke rising to vanish in the windswept branches above the flames.

He led his horse down an incline to a brook that ran between frost-cracked boulders, where he filled his canteen with the icy water in which darting crawfish stirred up a mixture of sand and mud from the brook's uneven bottom. He let the horse drink its fill, since he would be doing no more riding that night. Then he led the animal back up the incline and under the trees.

As the dun began to browse the thick shrubbery, Sutton took an oilcloth-wrapped package from his saddlebag and carried it over to the fire, where he sat down crosslegged on the ground and opened it. He feasted on fragrant goat cheese and thickly crusted bread which he had bought before leaving Virginia City. He washed the food down with water from his canteen.

When he had satisfied his hunger, he rewrapped what was left of the cheese and bread in the oilcloth and returned them to his saddlebag. His dun paid no attention to him as it continued to browse. He stripped his saddle, bedroll, and other gear from the horse and then draped his saddle blanket over a low-hanging branch to dry out. Then, taking an iron picket pin from his saddlebag, he drove it into the ground with the heel of his boot and fastened the dun's reins to it.

Back at the fire again, he welcomed its warmth because the night grew cold at the elevation he had reached, even though it was midsummer. He sat with his hat tilted back on his head to reveal the pale skin that began about an inch above his eyebrows and reached to his hairline, which was in sharp contrast to the bronze color of the rest of his face.

Nearby a poor will whipped in the darkness, a bleak sound. The wind continued to weave its way among the aspens. The light of the rising quarter moon was held at bay by their branches but beyond the trees the land was awash in silvery light. To Sutton, his horse looked, as it stood in the moonlight that gave the animal's hide a glow, more like the ghost of a horse than a real one.

He watched the fire burn slowly down, thinking of Jimmy Lee Cranston and remembering the time that he too, like Jimmy Lee now, had spent lonely nights and days almost as lonely in a jail in Texas for a murder he hadn't committed. I know how the boy feels, he thought. Friendless. Not able to bring himself to believe that this could really and truly be happening to him. That he might actually hang for a crime he didn't commit. Believing that something or somebody would step in to save him maybe at the last minute, believing that it was just not possible that he could die by mistake with so many of his allotted years unlived.

But it is possible, he thought grimly. Which proves that in some ways life, not to mention death—is a far piece from fair. He looked up at the sky, at the stars glittering in it, and felt his customary sense of awe at the impressive sight. Everything appears to be in good order, he thought. The moon's out night riding. It looks like it's riding herd on the stars. Maybe it's only when men get to mucking about with things that, for all their good intentions, things go wrong. Like they've done for Jimmy Lee Cranston.

He rose and got his bedroll. After spreading his tarp on the ground, he took off his cartridge belt and hat and placed them on the ground. Then, wrapping himself in his blanket, he lay down on the tarp, unholstered his six-gun and placed it next to him. He was asleep in a matter of minutes.

Late the next day Sutton arrived at the cabin and much larger barn behind it that was his destination. He drew rein some distance from where the two buildings sat in a clearing fringed with tree stumps just on the edge of the stage road. He studied the buildings, noting the rough-hewn wooden sign in front of the cabin that bore two painted words: MORRISON'S FREIGHTING.

No smoke came from the cabin's stone chimney. There was no sign of anyone in the immediate vicinity.

An uneasiness took hold of him. He began to wonder if he had made the trip for nothing. He tried to ignore the feeling as he stepped down from the saddle. Leaving his dun with the reins trailing, he made his way to the cabin door. He knocked on it and waited. Knocked again. No answer. He tried the door. Finding it unlocked, he opened it and went inside, his right hand resting on the butt of his .45.

The cabin was rudely furnished with crude wooden furniture that was obviously handmade. It had a dirt floor that clearly had not been swept in some time. Its single window was open, its glass panes filthy. Sutton hunkered down and felt the ashes in the hearth. Cold. He got up and looked around. There was an unmade rope bed against one wall. Against the opposite wall was a similar bed with a brown blanket neatly covering it.

He opened the door of the room's single cupboard. He found some weevil-infested flour in a tin with no top on it on one shelf of the cupboard and a crumpled-up bag that had once held Arbuckle's coffee on another.

He left the cabin and went to the barn. Empty. No

horses. No mules. No wagons. Outside again, he considered his next move. There was no way to know when Morrison would return. It could be days or even weeks. He could stay and wait for the teamster to return. But he knew he could not stay long. Because Jimmy Lee was soon to hang—in less than two weeks now. Sutton cursed the absent Morrison and then himself for being a chaser of wild geese.

Then he went to his horse and swung into the saddle, intending to head for the town of Ironbound, which he knew was only a few miles further along the stage road. Ironbound wasn't much of a town, but there just might be somebody there, he thought, who could tell him where Morrison was and when he would return. Maybe the teamster wasn't far away. Maybe he could still track him down in time. He turned his horse and headed west. He had gone no more than a mile when he saw a rider coming his way in the distance. The man was briefly silhouetted against the sun as he topped a rise and then started down through a treelined pass. The rider sank from sight as he descended, seeming to blend in with the hill behind him.

Maybe I'll get lucky, Sutton thought, and that'll turn out to be Morrison. But, as he came closer to the rider who had reappeared, he quickly realized that it wasn't Morrison, although he had never seen the teamster. But he had seen a picture of Dennis Rutledge and the man coming toward him on a gray was, without a doubt, Rutledge.

Sutton, excitement surging within him, drew rein. As Rutledge rode up to him, he said, "I see you were in Ironbound for supplies." He pointed to the bulging gunnysack tied to Rutledge's saddle horn.

Rutledge smiled and said, "I was. And just in time to

keep myself from starving to death. I'm afraid I'm not much of a housekeeper. I never think to replenish my supplies until I've run out of everything edible or it's gone bad on me."

"I take it you've set up housekeeping back at Morrison's place."

Rutledge frowned. He kneed his gray and the animal moved out in an easterly direction.

"Hold on," Sutton said, turning his dun and riding after Rutledge.

"Who are you, Deputy?" Rutledge asked nervously. "What do you want with me?"

"My name's Luke Sutton and I've got a subpoena in my pocket with your name on it, Rutledge. I'm taking you back to Virginia City on the strength of that subpoena, but first I want to ask you a couple of questions."

"About what?"

Sutton heard the nervous edge that suspicion had given to Rutledge's voice. He answered, "About the murder of Seth Grant. I understand you were there when Grant got it. What I want to know is what you saw happen that night."

"Why?"

"I've been hired to find you and Hank Tully and Etta Spode and learn what really happened that night."

"What do you mean 'what really happened that night'?" Rutledge asked edgily. "Jimmy Lee Cranston accused Grant of cheating him at cards and then the kid got Grant's gun and killed him with it. That's what really happened."

"Were you the one by any chance who slugged Jimmy Lee on the back of the head and knocked him out cold?" Sutton suddenly asked, his question a whiplash aimed at Rutledge.

Rutledge blanched. His lips parted, but no words came from between them. Suddenly, he slammed his heels into his gray's flanks and the horse bounded forward, bearing him swiftly away.

Sutton went after him, his hand going for his gun as he did so. He had it unleathered and was taking aim at Rutledge before he realized what he was doing. He had acted almost instinctively, but he hadn't fired, realizing in time that to shoot his quarry would not serve his purpose. Rutledge dead won't do me one bit of good, he told himself as he holstered his gun and urged his dun into a furious gallop.

He was passing Morrison's place with Rutledge still increasing the distance between them when he caught a badly blurred glimpse of a figure moving between Morrison's cabin and the barn. The figure vanished as Sutton galloped on in pursuit of Rutledge.

He rode past twisted, because they were steadily wind-whipped, junipers growing up out of what appeared to be naked rock and then into some tall timber, mostly lodgepole pine, as Rutledge changed direction and left the stage road. The hooves of Sutton's dun sent several alpine chipmunks scurrying for cover. He barely noticed their hectic flight as he kept his eyes—or tried to—on the mounted man up ahead of him. But Rutledge dodged through the timber, seeming to increase his speed rather than slow it because of the trees surrounding him.

Sutton again went for his gun. This time, taking careful aim, he squeezed off a shot and silently exulted when he saw that he had hit the low-hanging branch of the lodgepole pine he had been aiming at. The tree loomed just ahead of Rutledge, and the branch, broken off by Sutton's shot, dropped down to strike Rutledge on the head and shoulders as he rode beneath the tree, causing him to lose his grip on the reins. His gray faltered, then began to slow.

Before Rutledge could recover from the blow he had received from the falling branch, Sutton had caught up with him. With his gun still in his hand and aimed at Rutledge, Sutton ordered him to turn around.

"You intend to shoot me?"

"If I meant to shoot you, Rutledge, you'd have been dead a long time ago. No, I don't mean to shoot you, but I warn you I will if you try to give me the slip one more time. Now, let's go."

Rutledge meekly turned his horse and headed back through the timber with Sutton riding right behind him. When they reached the stage road, they turned west. Later, when they reached Morrison's cabin, both men dismounted. Leaving their horses behind them, they went inside the cabin where Rutledge dropped wearily into a chair.

Looking up at Sutton, he asked, "How did you find me?"

"Your wife mentioned to me that you used to partner with Morrison. Ed Munch at the dry goods store told me Morrison had bought some clothes too small for him. I figured they might be for you. They were, weren't they?"

Rutledge nodded. "Is Mary—my wife—all right?"

"She wasn't sickly when I saw her, but I know from what she said to me that she'd be a whole lot better off were you back with her in Virginia City where you belong."

Rutledge hung his head.

"Why did you run?" Sutton asked him.

"I didn't run. I just decided to get away from things

for a while. I felt like things were closing in on me. I'd never been mixed up in a murder before. I wanted some time alone."

"Maybe that's why Etta Spode and Hank Tully lit a shuck too. Do you reckon that's so?"

"Ask them."

"I can't do that on account of I don't know where they are."

Rutledge hesitated a moment and then, looking up at Sutton, asked, "If I tell you where Tully is, will you let me be?"

"You know where Tully is?"

"I'll tell you where he is if you'll let me be. Is it a bargain?"

Sutton stepped up to Rutledge. He seized the man by the shirt and dragged him to his feet. "Tell me where Tully's at!" he barked.

Rutledge shook his head. "Not unless you agree to get out of here and leave me alone."

Sutton slammed Rutledge up against the cabin wall, knocking over a heavy table as he did so. "Where's Tully?" When Rutledge remained silent, Sutton slammed him against the wall a second time, making sure this time that Rutledge's head struck it.

Rutledge let out a cry of pain. "I'll tell you. Don't do that again. Please don't."

"Where's Tully?"

"I ran into him on my way here. He was in Painted Rock. That's a town about five miles northeast of here. Now, let me go. We made a bargain."

"I made no bargain with you," Sutton contradicted Rutledge. But he released his hold on the man who went back to his chair and sat down.

"Look, Rutledge," Sutton said, "don't you realize

that a boy who says he's innocent is going to hang if I can't find proof that he didn't kill Grant? Do you want that hanging over your head for the rest of your life? Can you live with that?"

Rutledge moaned. "Why won't you just go away and leave me alone?"

"On account of I need to know which one of the three of you killed Seth Grant that night. Was it Etta Spode? Tully? You?"

Terror leaped in Rutledge's eyes. "I didn't do it! I swear to you that I didn't!"

"Did Etta Spode kill Grant?" Sutton pressed on. "Or was it Hank Tully?"

Rutledge shuddered as he tried to meet Sutton's piercing gaze but failed to do so. Looking away, he said, "You win. I give up. I'll tell you the truth. It wasn't—"

Before Rutledge could utter another word, a shot exploded through the open window behind Sutton.

As Sutton dived for cover behind the thick top of the overturned table, his hand going for his gun, whoever was outside the window fired at him but missed. Sutton swiftly returned the fire and then waited, his body tense, his eyes on the window, for the next shot. It never came.

When he heard the sound of a horse galloping outside the cabin, he ran for the door, threw it open and, gun in hand, peered cautiously around the doorjamb. He saw no one, but he could still hear the sound of pounding hooves fading away in the distance.

He was about to go after whoever it was that had fired through the window, but a groan from behind him stopped him in his tracks. He turned and looked down at Rutledge, who was sprawled face down on the floor with a ragged red hole between his shoulder blades.

FIVE

Sutton went to where Rutledge lay and hunkered down beside the wounded man. When Rutledge made no more sounds and didn't move, Sutton, fearing the worst, placed two fingers on the side of the man's neck. He was relieved to find a pulse, albeit a weak one, there.

Gently, he turned the man on his side and then on his back. He stared down at the small, almost neat entrance wound in Rutledge's chest, which contrasted sharply with the larger, bloodier exit wound in his back.

Rutledge's eyes were closed, and when Sutton spoke his name, they did not open.

Sutton holstered his gun and glanced at the open door. He badly wanted to go out after whoever it was who had shot Rutledge and tried to shoot him as well, but he did not want to leave Rutledge. A bubble of blood bloomed between Rutledge's partially opened lips. Got him in the lung, Sutton thought, as frothy spittle eased from Rutledge's mouth and flowed down his chin.

"Mary," Rutledge said, his wife's name a soft sigh in the still air of the room.

Sutton watched his eyes open and stare uncomprehendingly up at him. "Who was it shot you, Rutledge, do you know?"

"Am I—going—to die?"

"You're hurt bad."

Rutledge turned his head to one side and then looked back at Sutton. "It's so—so damned funny."

Sutton said nothing, not understanding what thought might lie behind Rutledge's words.

"I minded my business all my life," Rutledge whispered. "Never did harm to anyone if I could help it. It's funny that a man like me could get himself mixed up in a murder."

"Murder's never funny," Sutton said solemnly. "Neither is being mixed up in it."

"You're right—about that. I thought it would all blow over in time. I came here—got Morrison to buy some clothes for me to use. I—meant to go back—after it was all over but—"

As Rutledge's words faded away, Sutton saw the wounded man's eyes slip out of focus. He's going to die on me, he thought. Sure as shooting, he is. A sense of alarm, almost one of desperation, swept over him. If Rutledge dies before he can tell me what happened the night of Grant's murder, he thought, it'll cut my odds of saving Jimmy Lee by a third.

"Rutledge," he said, "you were going to tell me—"

". . . said we'd die if we didn't."

Sutton leaned closer to Rutledge as the man's voice faded. "I don't understand. Who said—"

"I was afraid. Not for me. For Mary—the baby." Rutledge's eyes closed.

Sutton gripped his shoulder, squeezed it. "Rutledge?"

"—our first baby. We hoped for—boy."

"Who shot you, Rutledge? Who shot Seth Grant?"

"—has killed me."

Rutledge's eyes opened and he stared wildly up at Sutton. He tried desperately to speak but Sutton heard only a wheeze, no words. Then Rutledge said, "—will kill you too."

"Who will? Dammit, Rutledge, *tell me!*" Sutton, despite his feelings of regret over what he believed to be Rutledge's imminent demise, wanted to shake the man, wanted to do something—anything he could—to force Rutledge to reveal what he knew before it was too late. But he did nothing but continue to hunker down beside the dying man and Rutledge struggled to breathe, his chest rising and falling, his face grimacing with the pain the effort caused him.

"Who killed Seth Grant?" Sutton asked for a second time and then, when he received no response, he repeated the question in a louder tone that bordered on a shout.

Rutledge sighed wetly. "Etta," he murmured. Then he died, his head lolling limply to one side, his eyes staring sightlessly.

Sutton swore and slammed a fist into his other hand as frustration born of disappointment welled up in him. Despite the fact that Rutledge had seemed to answer his question concerning the identity of Grant's killer, he couldn't be absolutely sure that Rutledge, by uttering Etta Spode's name, had, in reality, actually answered the question. Perhaps, Sutton speculated darkly, he had meant to say something that was in no way connected to what I asked him. Maybe he never even heard the last question I put to him. He swore again.

All I know for sure, he thought, as he stared down at the dead Rutledge, is that now there are only two people left who might be able to help me keep Jimmy Lee Cranston's neck out of a noose.

He went to the door, looked out, saw no one, heard

nothing. He left the cabin and went to the barn, where he found a shovel.

Later, after burying Rutledge, he retrieved the gunnysack that contained the supplies Rutledge had bought in Ironbound, and proceeded to cook himself a meal consisting of bannocks, which he made with cornmeal, and coffee.

Whoever it was killed Rutledge, he thought as he ate, did it to shut him up, to keep him from telling me what happened the night Grant was killed. He thought over what Rutledge had said.

You win. I give up. I'll tell you the truth. It wasn't—

And, he thought, whoever it was tried to kill Rutledge tried to kill me too, no doubt to keep me from talking to Etta Spode or Hank Tully—if it wasn't one of that pair who did the shooting just now. He glanced at the window. Whoever it was, he thought, had been listening to Rutledge and me talk through that open window. When Rutledge said he'd tell me the truth, that's when the shooting started. He suddenly recalled the barely glimpsed figure he had seen as he passed the Morrison cabin in pursuit of the fleeing Rutledge. He hadn't gotten a good look at whoever it was. All he could recall was that the figure—he didn't even know if it was a man or a woman—had been standing between the cabin and the barn. The bushwhacker? Maybe so.

When he had finished his meal, he cleaned the griddle he had used and then left the cabin. Outside, he boarded his dun and then, leading Rutledge's gray, he rode northeast, heading for the town of Painted Rock and, he hoped, Hank Tully.

It was dark when he arrived in Painted Rock, which was a young town, judging by the few board buildings and numerous canvas tents of which it was composed.

He rode down the winding dirt road that bisected the town until he came to a tent with a sign outside it which announced that it was a livery.

He dismounted and went inside, blinking in the bright light of the lanterns that illuminated the tent's interior, and said to the sleepy farrier he found there, "I've got a horse I want to board here and another one I'd like to sell to you if you're in the market to buy."

"I can always use good horseflesh," the farrier said. "Let's have a look at what you've got to offer me."

Sutton went outside and returned leading the two horses. "This one's for sale," he declared, indicating the gray. "He's sound enough. He's got good legs and a nice broad brisket. His eyes are clear and his teeth are good."

The farrier thumbed open the horse's lips and examined its teeth and then ran his hands over the horse's body. "Eight dollars," he offered when he had completed his examination of the animal.

"He's worth fifteen easy," Sutton countered.

Five minutes later, the two men had settled on a price of eleven dollars, which the farrier gave Sutton before leading the two horses to the stalls and feed bins set up in the rear of the tent.

Sutton left the livery and went to the road ranch that bore a sign that said: LODGINGS. He paid for a bed and bought some writing paper and a stamp from the proprietor of the place, who told him in response to his question that mail was brought to and picked up at Painted Rock by a mule train that brought in supplies once a week.

Sutton ducked under the hanging canvas that hid the sleeping area from the rest of the road ranch, and using a lantern given him by the proprietor, found himself an empty bed. Then, as sleeping men snored all around him, he wrote a brief letter to Mary Rutledge, telling her what had happened to her husband and expressing his sincere regrets over the man's death. He enclosed the eleven dollars he had received from the farrier for Rutledge's horse.

In the morning, after Sutton had given his stamped letter to the proprietor of the road ranch and asked him to mail it for him, he said, "I'm looking for a man name of Hank Tully. Do you know where I might find him?"

"Never have heard the name," was the proprietor's bored response.

Sutton nodded his acknowledgment of the disappointing answer and left the road ranch. Once outside, he surveyed the town that had, he thought, a temporary look about it—as if it might blow away in the next big wind or be buried in the first of the mountains' regular September blizzards. His gaze fell on the livery.

He smiled. If ever there was a storehouse of information masquerading under the name of gossip, the livery in a town was it, he knew. Still smiling, he recalled how his ma, when the family went to town on Saturdays, would always order him in no uncertain terms to stay away from the livery barn.

"I won't have my son turned into a livery barn bum," she would say sternly. "Just as sure as I know a saloon man is bound for hell, so do I know that a livery barn loafer will be right behind him with one hand on his shoulder."

Remembering now, Sutton continued smiling. He saw himself as he was then—eager to stand with feigned nonchalance in front of the livery barn with the older boys and the many men, spitting tobacco juice as they did and pretending to be not one bit shocked at the bawdy stories the men told, which would turn a preacher as pale as milk were he to hear them.

He studied the men of assorted ages who were gathered in front of the livery tent, most of them seated on an assortment of crates and boxes. That's the place for me to go to find out about Tully, he told himself. A town's livery's like a clubhouse. What's more, anybody who comes to town goes there and anybody leaving town also goes there. He remembered having picked up messages from friends left for him in livery barns down through the years. He remembered the signs he had seen tacked to the walls of livery barns which offered a plow for sale or told of a vigilance committee meeting to be held at someone's farm. He also remembered seeing in one livery barn in a long ago but not forgotten town in Texas, a dodger with his name on it and the offer of a reward for his capture dead or alive.

His thoughts drifted back to that ugly time. He thought of his brother, Dan, and how Dan had died—killed by the four men he had spent nearly as many years tracking down, one by deadly one. With an effort of will, he set those dark thoughts aside and strode down the street. When he reached the livery, he greeted the assemblage of men with an amiable "Howdy" and took a seat on a wooden cracker barrel.

A few nods and a muttered "How do" greeted him. The conversation that had been taking place before he arrived continued without interruption.

"Sure, I'm willing to admit that a man *can* make a crop up here in the mountains," one middle-aged man drawled as he whittled a stick and shavings piled up at his feet. "He can if he's patient and persevering. But I'll tell you boys this. Doing it's a hard fight with a mighty short stick."

A man near the speaker laughed and poked the man next to him in the ribs. Then, jerking a thumb in the direction of the man who had just spoken, he remarked, "Bill there's nothing but a possum farmer, so there ain't no use paying him no mind when he takes to fretting over his poor farm. You'd sooner catch him out with his rifle after varmints than walking behind a plow any day of the week."

Someone else said, "Did you happen to see Mrs. Molene in the road ranch last Saturday night? Even with her husband right there in plain sight she was giving every man present the glad eye."

"I hear," yelped an obviously overwrought young man, his eyes alight, "that Mrs. Molene can be pretty free with her favors when her hubby ain't nearby."

"What's the difference if other men than her husband have had at her?" said the man who had brought up the subject. "A slice off an already cut loaf ain't never going to be missed."

Sutton sat and listened to the idle ebb and flow of the talk that ranged from the dubious merits of one man's coon hounds to the high price of tobacco that some-body said wasn't worth buying, since it had no more bite than "a toothless old granny woman."

"Where you from, stranger?" a man standing next to Sutton asked him.

"Virginia City," he replied.

"You're a lawman, I see," the man remarked, and to Sutton it seemed that the eyes of all the men flicked to the badge he was wearing and then away from it.

"I am," he admitted, hoping that they would continue to question him, hoping that their curiosity about him would help him get the information he wanted about Hank Tully.

"We don't get many lawmen out this way," the man said, and another one added, "That deputy must be hunting somebody or other," as if Sutton were not there to hear him.

"Would that be the case?" a man asked Sutton.

"I'm looking for a man name of Hank Tully," he answered. He noted the glances exchanged in what seemed to him to be a suspicious manner. "He's wanted for questioning in Virginia City about a murder that happened there," Sutton added and was pleased at the wide-eyed expressions his words caused to appear on every one of his listeners' faces.

"Told you, Orville," one of the men said to a companion who was wearing a worn pair of bib overalls. "That fellow was up to no good. I knew it the minute I laid the first eye on him. He had the look of a killer about him. Remember those mean-spirited eyes of his?"

"Oh, go on with you, Oscar," chided Orville. "You're always ready to think the worst of everybody."

"He had the eyes of one of the devil's own," Oscar insisted heatedly.

"Beg pardon, gents," Sutton interrupted and all eyes turned to him again. "Are you talking about Hank Tully by any chance?"

"I am," declared Oscar and, simultaneously, "We are," from Orville.

"He's here in town, is he?" Sutton prompted.

"Nope," Orville replied. "He's been gone for—how long has that lowlife been gone, Oscar?"

"Two, three days," Oscar answered. "Who'd he kill, Deputy?"

Sutton sidestepped the question by asking one of his own. "What can you tell me about him?"

"He come to town on foot," Orville volunteered. "He said his horse give out on him. But he managed to get himself another one, he did, which he will probably kill too if I'm any judge of men. He was a man in a hurry."

Snickers, a noisy tide, rippled among the men, one of whom said, "And we all know how he got himself that new horse of his, don't we, boys?"

One of the men leaned close to Sutton, winked, shook a finger in Sutton's face, and intoned in a melodramatic voice, "It was the woman who come to town with him that got the both of them whatever they needed from the horse to beds over in the road ranch to meals over at the slop house yonder."

Sutton could barely contain his excitement. "There was a woman with Tully?"

"A tart," said Orville.

"A fancy woman," amended Oscar.

More snickers.

"She was always at him while they was here," Orville said. "She wanted to light out for someplace else. She didn't have no use for Painted Rock. I myself heard her call it a 'backwater.'"

"A woman like that," said one of the men with a gleam in his eyes, "needs bright lights and lots of fiddle music if she's to get even halfway home to contentment."

"Do any of you gents know where the two of them went?" Sutton asked, almost holding his breath.

"Well," said the man standing next to Sutton, "from what I heard they decided to go on to Gideon."

"That's a town west of here, as I recall," Sutton said.

"That's right," the man said. "It's bigger than Painted Rock. It's got itself two saloons to our one road ranch with women like the one Tully had with him falling out their doors and windows both."

"You ought to know," a man jibed, poking the man who had just spoken to Sutton in the ribs. "You've gone there often enough with your tongue hanging out so that it was slapping up against your knees."

"That wasn't my tongue," the man said with a lewd grin.

"Can any of you gents tell me," Sutton asked, "what Tully and the woman with him looks like so I'll recognize them if and when I catch up with them?"

Oscar answered, "Look for a man with a lot of brown hair but hardly any forehead. With a sunburned face and hands. Eyebrows that meet and shake hands right above his hawk's beak of a nose. And eyes that would scare Satan himself."

Orville, in a dreamy faraway voice, said, "The woman was about twenty or so years old. She had frizzy hair the color of the sun shining on wheat. She had a baby doll's China blue eyes, and oh, my, skin that looked as soft as goose down though I never got to touch her.

"She was wearing a dress that had spangles on it and didn't get close enough to say hello to her knees. Hell, it hardly hid her hips. Red it was."

Sutton rose. "It's been nice talking to you, gents. I'm much obliged to you for the information you've been good enough to give me."

"You had yourself a good rest back there at that livery in Painted Rock," Sutton told his dun. "You're stepping nice and high today." He patted the animal's neck. "Feeling frisky, are you?"

The horse tossed its head and snorted.

Sutton turned and glanced over his shoulder. Then to the right and to the left. No sign of anybody, he thought, but that doesn't necessarily mean that there's not somebody following me.

He rode past a tall wall of rocks, skirting the huge pool of water that was formed by a waterfall which seemed to tumble down from the clouds themselves. In reality, it cascaded over the top of the rock wall far above him, sending showers of spray into the air as it did so. The sun turned the spray's droplets into red, yellow, and green jewels shining like other-worldly stars against the clear sky.

He made his way down into a narrow canyon that was floored with a thick stand of larkspur. A sudden clattering above him made him go for his gun and look up. But it was not the sound of a horse's hooves on rock that he had heard but the hooves of a bighorn ram that was standing on the rimrock looking down at him, its hide and horns the same dun color as his horse.

His hand left the butt of his gun as he rode out of the canyon. He ducked as a swarm of bees suddenly engulfed him on their way to the larkspur that was in full purple bloom behind him on the canyon floor. He muttered an oath as one of the bees stung him on the neck.

When the swarm had gone, he drew rein and dismounted. Pouring some water from his canteen on the ground, he mixed the water with earth to make a mud poultice. He smeared it on the spot where the bee had stung him, which was now a swollen lump of painful flesh.

By the time he came out of the wilderness onto the rutted dirt road that led to Gideon, the bee sting was still swollen but no longer painful. When the town that was his destination appeared around a bend in the road, he spat on his fingers and wiped the mud from his neck. He looked up at the sun that was directly ahead of him, judging the time to be about three o'clock in the afternoon.

As he rode into Gideon, he noted the two saloons that he had been told about by one of the men in front of Painted Rock's livery. The two establishments faced each other on either side of the street in which pigs wallowed, making travel circuitous if not precarious, like two gaudy gunfighters squaring off and ready to throw down on one another.

The saloon on the north side of the street called itself the Golden Nugget and the one on the south side of the street called itself the Empire. Sutton dismounted in front of the Empire and wrapped his reins around the hitchrail in front of the saloon.

Once inside, he found the place almost empty. Two men sat at a table near the bar doing more talking than drinking, and another man lounged at one end of the bar slowly twirling a bottle of beer between his hands. There was not a single woman to be seen.

Sutton made his way across the sawdust-strewn floor that was pockmarked with the brown stains of tobacco spat by men who had ignored the presence of strategically placed brass spittoons.

"Whiskey," he told the bar dog as he hooked one boot heel on the brass rail that ran the length of the oak bar. When the bar dog had placed a bottle and glass in front of him, he filled the glass and then put the bottle down.

The bar dog glanced from Sutton's badge to his face and back again. Sutton raised his glass, gave the man a silent toast, and drank. "I reckon things'll pick up after sundown," he commented.

"They generally do," the bar dog responded.

"That's when the ladies come downstairs, am I right?"

The bar dog nodded.

"I was just over in Painted Rock," Sutton volunteered, "and I heard some boys over there speak mighty highly of a lady they told me could be found in one of the saloons in town, although they neglected to say which one. I have a hankering to make her acquaintance."

"We got no laws here against what our hostesses do," the bar dog remarked pointedly. "And you've got no jurisdiction here in Gideon, lawman."

"That's right, I haven't," Sutton agreed. "I'm sorry you read me wrong. I'm just here looking to keep company with a lady name of Etta Spode."

The bar dog looked blankly at Sutton.

"The name don't mean anything to you?"

The bar dog shook his head. "Try the Golden Nugget across the street," he suggested.

"She's got frizzy hair, the lady I'm hoping to meet," Sutton persisted. "Blue eyes. She's about twenty years of age, I've been told."

"The only frizzy-haired lady we got boarding upstairs," said the bar dog, "is named Dolly."

"Then I reckon I'll have to do like you said and look for the lady over at the Golden Nugget." Sutton poured more whiskey in his glass and then proceeded to help himself to some slices of bread and thick slabs of roast beef which were part of the Empire's free lunch.

That night Sutton stood just inside the batwings of the Golden Nugget and surveyed the noisy crowd in the smoky barroom. In the midst of a boisterous group of men stood a woman, one hand perched archly on her hip, who had yellow hair. But it was straight, swirled about on the top of her head like meringue, and held in place by amber hairpins. And, Sutton noticed with a strong feeling of disappointment as he moved closer to her for a better look, she's got gray eyes and can't be younger than forty.

There were no other women in the place who fit Etta Spode's description. One or two of the men, Sutton noticed, did, in the most general way, fit the description of Hank Tully that he had been given except for the fact that they all had mild-mannered eyes which, according to his informants, Tully definitely did not have.

Sutton left the Golden Nugget and crossed the street to the Empire. He dodged out of the way to avoid being struck by a man who was thrown headfirst through the batwings into the middle of the street.

Inside, the Empire was a combination of a circus and a riot. A woman was dancing on top of a table, her skirt held high above her knees while men surrounded her, their jaws gaping and their hands eagerly reaching. Dust rising from the sawdust on the floor caused Sutton to cough and made it difficult to see clearly. Someone fired a pistol at the ceiling, causing wooden chips to rain down. Someone else sang at the top of his voice, his words badly slurred, his arms waving aimlessly. In a corner of the room, a man played the piano but only a note or two could be heard now and then above the din.

Sutton squinted into the smoke and dust, searching for Etta Spode and Tully. His eyes came to rest on a man at a table who was swiftly and skillfully dealing cards. That's him, Sutton thought, as he noted the dealer's narrow forehead, the way his eyebrows met above the bridge of his hooked nose, his sunburned face and hands, and, most importantly, his cold cruel eyes. That's Tully all right, he decided. There's not likely to be two men who have the stare of a snake like he's got.

He unpinned his badge and thrust it into his pocket. Then he shouldered his way through the crowd to stand directly behind the man he believed was Hank Tully, while he continued to scan the room, hoping to catch a glimpse of Etta Spode.

At his side, a wheel of fortune spun. On the far side of the room, a game of faro was in progress. Gaudily dressed and heavily powdered women moved among the tables, stopping to chat with a man now and then, sometimes taking the money the men offered before leading them up the stairs to the upper floor.

Sutton's eyes rose as the door of a room on the second floor balcony opened, and a woman stepped out and leaned against the wooden railing while she surveyed the scene below her. It's her, he thought, noting the woman's yellow frizzy hair, bright blue eyes, and red spangled dress that showed some signs of wear. He continued watching as she primped, one hand touching her hair, the other smoothing her bodice, and then turned and started down the steps.

He pushed his way through the crowd and managed to arrive at the foot of the stairs at the same time she did.

"Evening," he greeted her. "I'd like to buy you a drink."

The woman who so closely resembled the description he had been given of Etta Spode gave him a casual glance and then studied him more closely. "It's been awhile," she said, "since such a good-looking gent as yourself made me an offer. Mostly I get the culls, not the prime beef."

"Begging your pardon, miss, but I just can't get myself to believe that. What with your looks and"—his eyes dropped to her body—"charms—well, I think you're just trying to make a down-at-the-heels drifter feel good."

"Is that what you are? A drifter?"

"I've been on the move a lot lately."

"What's your name, drifter?"

It was time to get down to business, Sutton decided. "Luke Sutton," he answered. "You're—"

"You can call me Dolly."

For a moment, Sutton was taken aback but then he quickly decided that "Dolly" was just a name Etta Spode had adopted to hide behind, a ploy he himself had used at times in the years gone by.

"What about that drink, drifter?"

Her words brought him back to the here and now. He offered her his arm and led her over to the bar where, as a result of some pushing and shoving on his part, he managed to make room for both of them. "What will you have?" he asked her.

"A little white wine," she told him and he ordered for both of them.

When they had their drinks, they touched glasses, the clink lost in the cacophony surrounding them, and drank.

"Are you looking for a good time?" she asked Sutton.

He was about to say no when he thought it might be easier to talk to her in a place that was quieter, and her room upstairs, he suspected, would be at least a little bit quieter than where they were.

"I am," he said. "How much does a good time cost?"

"Five dollars. More if you want to spend the night."

"Sounds good to me."

She took his hand and led him through the crowd, up the stairs, and into the room he had seen her emerge from earlier.

SIX

After closing the door, Sutton said, "There's no point in my beating about the bush any longer. I have to tell you I know you're Etta Spode."

The woman standing beside the bed gave him a defiant look. "So what if I am?"

"I came here hunting you. You and Hank Tully."

Etta's defiant glare dissolved into an expression which blended surprise and dismay. "What business do you have with me?" she snapped. "Or with Hank Tully, for that matter?"

"Lawman's business." Sutton took his badge from his pocket and showed it to Etta.

"I haven't broken any law," she said. "Neither has Hank."

"I don't recollect saying you did," he countered as he pinned his badge back on his vest.

"Then what—"

"I've got subpoenas in my pocket for you and Tully which means I'm taking you both back to Virginia City with me to talk to Sheriff Cobb about the murder of Seth Grant—after you talk to me about the same thing."

"Jimmy Lee Cranston killed Seth with Seth's own gun which Jimmy Lee took from him." Etta paused, studying Sutton. "You look like you don't believe me."

"The plain fact of the matter is I don't."

"Then why don't you go ask Hank or Dennis Rutledge what happened. They'll tell you the same story, see if they don't."

"I can't ask Rutledge. He's dead."

Etta searched Sutton's face as if she were trying to determine whether or not he was telling her the truth. "Dead?" she repeated softly.

"Somebody bushwhacked him—him and me along with him. The somebody killed Rutledge but, as you can see, didn't manage to do the same for me. I wouldn't be one bit surprised if that somebody doesn't come gunning for you and Tully too."

"Why?"

"I can't say for certain. But if I had to guess I'd say that somebody is trying to get rid of the eyewitnesses to the killing of Grant."

"That's ridiculous. Why would anyone want to do that, for heaven's sake?"

"I told you I don't know if that's why Rutledge was killed, not for sure I don't, but I'm telling you what happened so that you can go about being safe rather than sorry in case that same somebody comes after you and Tully."

"I'm not afraid."

"Maybe you should be. A little fear puts a sharp edge on a man—or woman. Now, I have a question for you. Is that Hank Tully downstairs dealing cards—the jasper with the mean-as-murder eyes and brown bush of hair?"

"Yes, that's Hank. Are you going to arrest us?"

"No, I don't reckon there'll be any need for that. I just want to hear you two tell me what happened the night Grant got it. Now, you sit tight right here and I'll go get Tully and then the three of us, we'll talk."

Sutton left the room but was back with Tully in tow within five minutes.

"What the hell's this all about, Etta?" Tully barked as he entered the room. "What's this lawdog doing here?"

Before Etta could reply, Sutton closed the door and said, "I told you downstairs, Tully, that I've got a subpoena for you and that the three of us had to have a talk. Now, what we're going to talk about is who killed Seth Grant."

"Jimmy Lee Cranston killed him," Etta said.

"We both saw him do it," Tully added. "Me, Etta, and a fellow named Rutledge who was also there that night saw the kid cut him down."

"Rutledge is dead," Sutton said and then told Tully what he had earlier told Etta about the bushwhacking at Morrison's cabin.

Etta sat down on the edge of the bed as Tully leaned back to brace his buttocks against the windowsill.

"Jimmy Lee was in a rage that night," Etta announced, looking at the floor. "I've never seen anybody so mad. He had lost money at cards to Seth whom he accused of cheating him."

"When Grant wouldn't give the kid back the money he'd lost," Tully said, folding his arms across his chest, "the kid just up and jumped him, got his gun away from him, and drilled him twice."

"Three times," Etta quickly corrected Tully. "Jimmy Lee shot Seth three times," she added for emphasis, glancing at Sutton as she did so.

"Have you got a poor memory, Tully?" Sutton inquired casually.

"Who remembers everything after all this while?" Tully shot back angrily. "Two, three times, what's the difference? Grant's dead and his killer's set to hang or so I hear."

"He won't though," Sutton said firmly. "Not if I can help it, he won't." He paused for a thoughtful moment. Then, "Jimmy Lee said it was you, Tully, who hit him on the back of the head," he lied.

"It wasn't me!" Tully roared. "It was—"

"*Hank!*" Etta screeched, rising from the bed.

Tully looked in her direction. So did Sutton, and he saw now that there was fear in her eyes.

"Was it you who shot Grant, Etta?" he asked sternly.

"No!" she cried. "It wasn't me!"

"I asked Rutledge just before he died who had killed Grant, and he gave me your name," Sutton declared.

"Well, he was lying," Etta said in a shaky voice. "I didn't do it. And I'm not going to say anymore. Not one more word." She turned to Tully and the fear in her eyes was submerged briefly in fury. "And don't you open that big mouth of yours even once more, Hank Tully!" she practically screamed at him.

"All right, that's enough," Sutton said. He got to his feet. "The three of us are going to take a trip back to Virginia City. It's obvious to me that Tully, at least, knows that somebody did hit Jimmy Lee on the head like the boy's been claiming all along, so I reckon the sheriff and Jimmy Lee's lawyer—maybe the boy himself —ought to have a chance to ask you both some questions like I've just been doing. It might turn out that they'll hear even more interesting answers from Tully— maybe even from you too, Miss Spode—than any I've heard so far. Let's go."

Sutton started for the door. He never made it.

Tully sprang away from the windowsill and clubbed him on the side of his head with both fists. Sutton lost his balance and started to go down. As he did so, Tully struck him again, this time on the back of the head, with the butt of his gun. Sutton was unconscious before his body hit the floor.

Shifting shapes. Both bright and somber colors. Sounds which, as Sutton slowly regained consciousness, became words.

"Is he dead?"

"What happened?"

"Who is he?"

He blinked and saw that the shifting shapes were men and women surrounding him where he lay on the floor. They were peering down at him, some with mere curiosity, some with expressions of shock on their faces. The bright and somber colors were the flamboyant dresses of the women and subdued garb of the men.

He got an elbow under him, then another. A man held out a hand and helped him to his feet.

"Where are they?" he asked as somebody handed him his hat, which he had lost in the encounter with Tully.

"Who is it you're looking for?" one of the women asked him.

"Who laid you low?" a man asked him.

"I'll answer both your questions at the selfsame time," he told them. "The woman you folks call Dolly and a man named Hank Tully."

"I know Dolly," the woman said, "but I never heard of Hank Tully. Did any of you ladies or gents?"

Heads shook.

Sutton said, "He was dealing cards downstairs before I got him to come up here."

"I saw you with him," someone said. "But that fellow, he called himself Graham—Bill Graham."

"It doesn't matter what he called himself," Sutton said. "What does matter is where he is—him and the woman whose real name, by the way, is Etta Spode."

"They both ran out of the place like their tails was on fire," said a man in the crowd.

"I thought that seemed funny," a woman said, "so I came up here to check Dolly's room and found you with your lights out."

"Where'd they go?" Sutton asked, clapping his hat back on his head. "Does anybody know?"

"I seen them," a man with his arm around the waist of one of the women volunteered. "I was on my way here when I seen them hightail it down the street and into the livery."

"I'm obliged to you folks," Sutton said and then hurried out of the room and down the steps. Once outside, he sprinted down the street to the livery.

He found no one inside it. I'll just have to leave some money to pay my horse's board and feed bill, he thought. I sure can't wait around for somebody to show up before I head out after Tully and his lady friend.

He was saddling and bridling his dun when the farrier he had met earlier appeared in the doorway and stopped dead in his tracks, his wary eyes on Sutton. As the man began to back away, Sutton flipped down his stirrups and said, "Hold on there. I'm not about to bite you. I'm just here collecting my horse."

The farrier relaxed and came inside.

Sutton stepped out of his dun's stall and said, "There was a woman and a man came in here not long ago, I'm told." He described Etta and Tully to the farrier.

"Yes, sir, they were here a little while ago. The man,

he pulled a gun on me and stole a cinnamon buckskin. His own horse was here too. Him and the woman rode in on it together, but I heard him say to her that riding double now would slow them down too much. When I come in just now and seen you here, I guess I spooked on account of what had just happened here with those horse thieves."

"Which way did that pair go when they rode out, did you see?"

"Yes, sir, I did. They rode out on the north side of town."

"How much do I owe you for feeding and keeping my mount?"

After settling his bill, Sutton led his dun out of the livery. As he stepped into the saddle, clouds slid swiftly across the sky, obliterating the moon and all the stars.

It's about as black as the pit, he thought as he rode out of town in a northerly direction. A night as dark as this one's no time to be cutting for sign.

But cut for it he did. Not far from the edge of town, he found, when the moon reappeared, the trail of two horses that had been traveling side by side. The trail veered suddenly in the direction of Painted Rock. If it's Etta and Tully's trail I'm following, he thought, maybe they decided to head back to where they maybe made themselves some friends who'll give them cover to help them try to shake me.

The moon vanished behind the clouds again, and the little light it had been shedding vanished with it, leaving Sutton unable to see clearly the trail he had been following. He drew rein, waiting for the moon to reappear. It didn't. What did appear was lightning which streaked across the sky. It was followed by the rumble of thunder and then by raindrops. Sutton swore, knowing he could do no more cutting for sign until the storm was over.

As the rain intensified, he reached for his slicker, which was tied behind his saddle along with his bedroll, and put it on. Pulling his hat down low on his forehead, he rode on, searching for cover.

He found it under an upward-slanting slab of tall rimrock which had enough room under it—barely—for him and his horse if they stayed close together and didn't move around very much. He dismounted and led his dun under the overhang. He left the animal standing there, its head facing the rock wall, its rump bearing the brunt of the storm. He hunkered down beneath the horse's head, his back braced against the rocky wall behind him which forced him, because of the fairly sharp angle of its upward slant, to bend forward until the brim of his hat was almost touching his dun's forelegs.

As the night wore on, the storm gained strength. Lightning struck a tree not far from Sutton's refuge. He heard, but could not see, a portion of it fall to the ground. The wind rose and sent the rain to invade his shelter. He bore it stoically, the collar of his slicker turned up and his head lowered to let his hat shield his face.

He awoke, surprised to find that he had fallen asleep despite the roar of the thunder and the keen whip of the wind-driven rain. The sky was beginning to brighten and, in the light of the false dawn, he saw the top third of the tree that had been struck by lightning lying on the ground not far away. Water dripped from tree branches, the body of his horse, and his slicker.

He got up and stretched to rid his body of the stiffness he felt. Then he led his dun out from under the overhang and over to a patch of short grass, where he let it graze as he cut for sign in the quickly brightening light of the new day. His boots made sucking sounds as he walked across bare spots of ground that had been turned boggy by the tempest of the night before. He found no sign of the trail he had been following before the moon had vanished and the storm began.

He went back to his dun, drank from his canteen, and tried to ignore the rumbling of hunger in his gut. When he felt that his horse had had enough to eat, he climbed into the saddle and rode out.

Maybe, he thought, I'll pick up the trail again once I get to a place where the storm didn't touch down. If I don't, I'll see if anybody's seen Etta or Tully back in Painted Rock.

The curved dome of a red sun appeared above an eastern hill. It flooded the valley below where Sutton had drawn rein and dismounted to pick pigweed. He ate the leaves of the plants and then resumed his journey. Some time later, he came upon a broad patch of wild strawberries—many were rotted but a few were still edible. The latter he picked and ate.

When he resumed his journey, he continued searching for signs of the trail he had lost but he found none. By the time he reached Painted Rock, the sun had set and he had a keen and disturbing sense of another day lost. He went directly to the livery and made inquiries, but the farrier there with whom he left his horse claimed to have seen no one answering the descriptions he gave of Tully and Etta. Neither had anyone at the town's road ranch. He checked the saloon but did not find his quarry, nor could he gain any information about them from the men and women he talked to about them.

He rented a bed at the road ranch for the night. He flopped down on it and lay with his hands clasped behind his head, staring up at the ceiling and seeing ghostly images of Tully and Etta looking down at him and laughing. The frustration that he was feeling, combined with the tension he also felt, which was a result of his sense of time passing swiftly, kept him awake for most of the night.

In the morning, after leaving the road ranch, he breakfasted in a restaurant near it. The food and the several cups of black coffee he drank banished to a degree the weariness his almost totally sleepless night had left him as an unwanted legacy.

He rode out of town, heading back the way he had come, knowing there was nothing else he could do. He would have to go back to the spot where he had lost the trail and try harder to find it. It was the only hope he had of tracking down his quarry. If he couldn't find the trail—he wouldn't let himself think about that ugly possibility.

It was late in the day when he reached the spot where he had lost the trail in the darkness of the previous night. Once again, after carefully surveying the ground in the area, he could find no trace of any trail.

He sat his saddle, tipped his hat back on his head, and wrapped his hands around his saddle horn. What now, he asked himself. The answer came quickly. If I couldn't pick up the trail again between here and Painted Rock and neither Tully nor Etta showed up there—or so I was told—there's only one other thing that could have happened and that's that they swerved somewhere, either to the right or the left. They couldn't have doubled back, else I'd have seen some sign that they did.

He rode to the right, his eyes on the ground and on the shrubbery growing all around him. He saw no broken or bent branches, no prints in the earth made by man, woman, or horse. He turned and rode back to the spot from which he had started and then beyond it for a mile.

He turned his dun and rode thirty yards from his path and then headed back the way he had come. When he was again about a mile beyond the trail he had followed to Painted Rock earlier, he repeated the process, crisscrossing the country as he continued his search.

The sun was down and shadows were lengthening and darkening when he heard a sound off to his left. He quickly drew rein and sat his saddle, listening carefully but hearing nothing. He had almost begun to believe that he had imagined the sound that he thought resembled a moan when he heard it again. His head swiveled to the side, and he peered in among the timber where shadows seemed to dash and dart about as a breeze stirred the branches of the trees. He walked his horse into the timber, his gun drawn, his eyes turned away from the dying light to sharpen his night vision.

He heard what he now was convinced was a moan for a third time. He dismounted, and easing back the hammer of his gun, headed cautiously toward the spot from which the sound had come. When he reached it, he found Hank Tully lying on his back on the ground with his eyes closed. Tully's right hand clutched the thin trunk of a cedar sapling while the fingers of his left hand feebly clawed at the ground.

Tully was still armed, Sutton noted, but obviously in no shape to draw, let alone fire, the weapon holstered on his hip. Leathering his own gun, Sutton got down on one knee beside Tully and spoke the man's name. It was not until he had uttered the name for a third time that Tully's eyes eased open and tried to focus.

"—almost—almost outran you," Tully said.

"What happened to you, Tully?" Sutton asked, seeing no wounds on Tully's body.

"—killed me," was Tully's almost inaudible answer.

"Who? How?"

"Knifed me—my back."

Sutton reached out with both hands and started to turn Tully over. The man let out a weak cry of pain. Sutton, moving the man as gently as he could, managed to turn him over. He felt his gorge rise at what he saw and what he smelled.

There were three puncture wounds in Tully's back, one just below the rib cage on the left side and two higher up on either side of the man's spine. Tully's shirt was stiff with crusted blood and stuck to the edges of all three wounds. The stench of corruption rose in waves to assault Sutton's nostrils as he stared with a feeling of revulsion at the fat white wormlike things which were twisting and squirming in the gaping red mouths of the three wounds on Tully's back.

"Who knifed you?" he asked Tully.

"Don't know him. He was on my backtrail—never noticed him—told me he meant to kill me—said he didn't trust me to keep my mouth shut anymore."

"Keep your mouth shut about what? About Grant's murder?"

"*Yessss.*" The word was a soft sibilance in the growing darkness. "It was the man who knifed me who did in Grant," Tully whispered. "He came bursting into Etta's place that night and shot Grant in cold blood. Jimmy Lee Cranston didn't kill Grant."

Sutton felt as if a great weight had been lifted from his shoulders. At last, he thought, I'm getting the true story. "Why did this man, whoever he is, kill Grant?"

"Don't know. He's the one clubbed Jimmy Lee to put him out and then he put Grant's gun in the kid's hand. He told us that night—me and Etta and Rutledge—to say it was Jimmy Lee who killed Grant if anybody ever asked us. Then he told us it would be wise if the three of us got out of town and stayed out until after Jimmy Lee was hanged, which would leave him in the clear. He told Rutledge if Rutledge didn't do what he said, he'd kill Rutledge's wife. Me he said he'd kill real slow and that's what he's gone and done to me. He caught up with me the morning after Etta and I gave you the slip back in Gideon. He ran off my buckskin and left me here for dead.

"He said he changed his mind and decided to get rid of all three of us." Tully paused, coughed, almost choked. Then he continued, "He said—said he should have done that in the first place and hung our murders on Jimmy Lee too, along with Grant's.

"He said he'd tracked down Rutledge at some freighter's place where he killed him. He said there was a lawman with Rutledge and he almost plugged him too. I reckon that lawman was you."

"It was me, all right. Where's Etta?"

"She left me a couple of hours before that killer ran me down. I wanted to head for California. She didn't. So we split up. She headed east. I don't know where she went. I do know she planned to head back to Virginia City once the kid had been hanged. I never should have let her tag along with me when I left Virginia City. But she begged me to take her with me. She said she didn't think she could make it on her own. I reckon it's a good thing she went her own way when she did on account of that bushwhacker. Before he stabbed me he asked me where she was, but I told him I didn't know, which was the gospel truth, but that I did know she'd planned to go back home to Virginia City once Cranston had been hanged. I reckon he's out hunting her right now, and when he catches up with her she'll be as dead as I am.''

"You're not dead yet, Tully. I mean to try my damnedest to see to it that you don't die on me so you can tell your story—the one you just told me about who really killed Grant—to the sheriff in Virginia City.''

But I'm no doctor, Sutton thought grimly, and maybe the man who stabbed Tully has done some damage I can't rectify.

"I'll patch you up and then get you to a doctor somewhere," he told Tully. "The first thing I got to do is clean out your wounds as best I can. There's maggots in them.''

"I know," Tully murmured with a grimace. "I've been feeling them eating at me. Oh, God in heaven, it's an awful bad feeling, a sick-to-the-stomach feeling.''

"You ought to be glad you got those maggots," Sutton said, getting to his feet. "They eat infected flesh, which helps clean wounds.''

He rose, and leaving Tully lying face down on the ground, proceeded to build a fire for light to see by. Then he got his canteen and knelt down again next to Tully. He pulled his bowie knife from his boot and, after unsheathing it, he began to cut away the parts of Tully's shirt that were stuck to the wounds.

Tully groaned. His flesh quivered. "Leave me be," he

muttered. "You're hurting me bad and I'm as good as dead anyway."

Sutton ignored him. He thumbed two cartridges from his belt, split them open with his knife, and poured the gunpowder they contained on the wounds where the maggots continued to feed. Taking a match from a cuff of his jeans, he struck it on his boot heel and told Tully to brace himself. Then he lit the gunpowder in each of the wounds.

As the gunpowder flared and began to burn, Tully screamed loudly and desperately tried to scramble away. But Sutton reached out and held him down with both hands. He watched as the maggots burned to death, their white bodies crackling and turning black in the three small fires he had built on Tully's body.

A moment later, when the flames had died, he used his knife to remove charred flesh and the crisped remains of the maggots from Tully's back. Tully had screamed when Sutton began his primitive surgery and then subsided into a helpless sobbing which, in turn, faded away into silence when Tully fainted in the face of his ordeal.

When Sutton was finished some time later, fresh blood was flowing from all three of Tully's wounds. He let it run to thoroughly cleanse the wounds and then, ripping off a piece of Tully's shirt, he soaked it in water from his canteen and used it to wash away the blood. Pressing the wet cloth to each of the wounds in turn, he held it in place until the blood had clotted.

Then he rose and gathered more wood, which he placed on the fire. He was sitting cross-legged on the ground beside the fire, which gave off a welcome warmth that partially dispelled the night's chill, when Tully regained consciousness and groaned.

"—can't hardly breathe," he rasped. "I hurt on the outside now about as bad as I do on the inside."

Sutton remained silent.

"I'll never make it back to Virginia City," Tully murmured, his eyes squeezed shut. "Which don't matter now anyhow."

"It matters to me that you make it," said Sutton sharply, "on account of how you're the one who's going to save Jimmy Lee's life."

"I'm not." Tully made a gurgling sound. A moment later, he vomited blood. When his desperate gasping for breath finally subsided, he said, "In my pocket—paper."

Sutton moved closer to Tully. He searched through the man's pockets until he found a folded piece of paper, which he withdrew.

"You're too late, lawman," Tully managed to gasp.

Sutton unfolded the paper and saw by the light of the flickering fire that he was holding a page from *The Territorial Enterprise* which was dated the day after he had left Virginia City.

"Got that off a drummer in Gideon," Tully said breathily. "It's got some news about the kid's hanging which is why Etta took a notion when she read it that it would soon be safe for her to head back to Virginia City."

Sutton didn't understand. Holding the newspaper close to the fire in order to be able to read it, he scanned the article headlined: CRANSTON TO DIE. What Tully had been referring to, he discovered, was in the article's second paragraph. Sutton felt cold despite his nearness to the fire as he read that Jimmy Lee Cranston's scheduled hanging had been moved up to—

The date included in the article caught and held Sutton's eye. Jimmy Lee, the paper reported, was scheduled to hang just two days from now at noon, the date of the execution having been moved forward by order of the court.

Two days.

The words echoed in Sutton's mind. I'll never get Tully back there in time to save Jimmy Lee, he thought. I'm not sure I could get back there myself were I riding alone. Toting a half-dead man I know I couldn't do it without killing him and my horse too.

SEVEN

Sutton quickly made up his mind.

"Tully"—he said, and as the man stirred slightly like a weary sleeper, he continued—"is there a doctor in Gideon or Painted Rock?"

"Not in Painted Rock. There's an over-the-hill sawbones in Gideon who should have been put out to pasture twenty years ago."

"I know it's going to be hard on you, Tully, but you're going to have to do some riding. I'll help you climb up behind me on my horse. You can hang on to me. I'll try to take it as easy as I can but I got to warn you it's likely to be a tough trip."

"You'll kill me for sure making me ride all the way to Gideon."

Sutton was aware that Tully might well be right. But he was also aware that he had no other choice. "I can't just leave you out here in the middle of no place," he told Tully somewhat harshly. "So come on. Let's get you aboard my mount."

It was a struggle. Sutton, after helping Tully to his feet, had to half-carry and half-drag the man to where his dun stood not far from the fire. When they reached the horse, a spasm shuddered through Tully's body, almost bending it double. But Sutton managed to get him up on the dun.

When Sutton was in the saddle, he told Tully to hold on to him and then he put heels to his horse and the animal moved out and into a gallop that left Tully swearing and swaying behind Sutton.

They had not gone a mile when Sutton felt Tully's grip on him relax. Minutes later, he felt the man's body bump up against his own.

"You all right?" he asked.

No response from Tully.

He considered slowing the pace of his dun but he didn't. I've got myself caught on the horns of one mean damn dilemma, he thought as he continued his journey, one hand held behind him to prop Tully up. If I ride too hard I run the risk of hurting Tully, maybe hurting him bad. But if I slow down I run the risk of not getting back to Virginia City in time to stop them from hanging Jimmy Lee.

When he felt Tully slip to one side, he gave the man a shove to straighten him up. "Once we get to the doctor at Gideon," he said, "he'll fix you up just fine, you'll see."

A sceptical grunt from Tully.

A moment later, Tully fell from the dun. He screamed when he hit the ground.

Sutton drew rein and dismounted. He went back to where Tully was lying, and gritting his teeth, a muscle in his jaw jumping, he again helped—forced—Tully back aboard his horse.

Tully cursed halfheartedly. He tried to hit Sutton with a fist he had barely the strength left to clench. Sutton easily swatted the feeble blow aside.

They rode on together, Tully's head resting between Sutton's shoulder blades.

When they had arrived in Gideon and Sutton had received directions to the doctor's house from the driver of a produce-laden wagon, he made his way there, his dun soaked with sweat, its head lowered as if in defeat.

He dismounted and as he did so Tully began to list. Sutton caught him, and wrapping Tully's left arm around his shoulder and putting his right arm around Tully's waist, he helped him up the steps and knocked on the doctor's door which bore a brass plaque that read: B. MCDEVITT, M.D.

The door was opened by a man Sutton estimated to be at least seventy and probably closer to eighty years old. He took one look at Tully and said to Sutton, "The mortician's over on the other side of town."

"Are you Dr. McDevitt?" Sutton inquired, and when the man nodded, he pushed past him as he wordlessly pointed to his office in answer to Sutton's questioning look. When Sutton laid his burden down on the doctor's examining table, he said, "This man—his name's Hank Tully—has been stabbed in the back three times. I cleaned up his wounds as best I could. But he's in bad shape."

"I can see that."

"I want to make sure he doesn't die, Doc. He's very important to me."

The doctor gave Sutton a questioning look.

"I'm a deputy sheriff from Virginia City and I've got a subpoena for this man. But he's in no shape to travel and I've got to get back to Virginia City in time to stop a hanging, which means I'll be riding rough and riding hard. He couldn't live through a ride like the one I've got facing me, so I'm going to leave him here for you to look after. When I've done what I have to do in Virginia City, I'll be back for him."

"Hold on one minute, Deputy," the doctor said. "I

don't do business that way. How do I know you'll come back? How do I know I'll get paid?"

Sutton thrust a hand into his pocket and came up with a double eagle. "Here's twenty dollars," he said, handing the gold coin to the doctor. "If it turns out I owe you more than that I'll pay you when I get back here to take Tully off your hands. If for any reason you want to get in touch with me before then you can send word to Sheriff Cobb in Virginia City. Which reminds me, have you got any law here in Gideon?"

The doctor shook his head.

"Then I'll have to hold you responsible for Tully. Keep him here till I get back."

"I'm no lawman," the doctor protested. "I don't even own a gun. How am I going to hold him if he makes up his mind to leave?"

"That's your problem, Doc. Tie him up. Give him an overdose of laudanum. Do whatever you have to do. But keep him alive and keep him here."

"I'm not making you any promises on that score, Deputy," the doctor said. "I want that understood. But I'll do my best for him."

Sutton fervently hoped that Dr. McDevitt's best would be good enough.

After leaving the doctor's office, Sutton led his dun to the Golden Nugget, where he bought a bottle of whiskey and then to the livery, where he asked the farrier for a bucketful of bran. When he had it, he removed the dun's bridle, poured some whiskey into the bucket, and mixed it by hand with the bran. As the horse lowered its head to eat, Sutton wiped his hand on his jeans and then stored his bridle and bottle of whiskey in his sad-

dlebag. Taking a braided hackamore from his saddlebag, he waited for the dun to finish its feed.

"You leaving him here?" the farrier asked, jerking a
thumb in the direction of Sutton's horse.

"Nope."

"Then how come you took his bridle off, if you don't
mind my asking?"

"I've got a hard and long ride ahead of me—all the
way to Virginia City, and I've got to make it in less than
two days, so I'm going to use this hackamore instead of
a bridle. I don't want any iron in my mount's mouth to
bloody it when the going gets rough, as it's bound to."

"Wondered what for you were dosing him with whiskey. I see now you want to be sure he's not going to be
feeling any pain when you've been on the trail awhile."

"That's it. Now, there's one other thing. I'm in need
of a clean and dry saddle blanket. Have you got one
you'll swap me for mine?"

"Be right back." When the farrier returned, he was
carrying an Indian blanket.

Sutton took it and then stripped his remaining gear
from the dun as it continued to eat the mash he had
prepared for it. He used his sweat-soaked blanket to
wipe down the horse and then he placed the new blanket the farrier had given him on its back. By the time he
had the dun saddled again, the animal had emptied the
bucket. He placed the hackamore on the dun's head,
adjusted it, and then turned over his wet blanket to the
farrier and settled his bill with the man.

Outside the livery, he stepped into the saddle and
kneed the dun first into a trot and then into a full gallop.
Seconds later, Gideon was far behind him.

He gave the dun free rein and, as he did so, he had
the disturbing feeling that something was wrong. At

first, he wasn't sure what it was but then it came to him. He heard no clinking of a bridle chain, a familiar sound he had become so accustomed to that he seldom noticed it. But now he had become aware of it by the fact of its absence.

As the sky brightened, he rode on, weaving his way around piles of boulders, making his way through high mountain meadows, and trying as he did so not to think of the very real possibility that he might reach his destination too late—after Jimmy Lee had been hanged for a murder he didn't commit.

The hairs on the nape of his neck prickled, and despite the warm rays of the sun on his body, he shivered. By mid-morning, the dun under him was riding rough. Its gait faltered and its ragged breath burst from its lungs in short wet sobs. Sweat ran in small streams down the animal's neck and withers to slick its hide and soak its mane.

By noon, Sutton knew he had no choice. He drew rein, and as the dun came to a shuddering halt, he began to lead his mount through the twisting canyon that was just ahead of them. He knew he was losing precious time but he also knew he had no choice but to walk the horse if he didn't want to kill it.

He definitely did not want to kill it. Without his horse, he would, he knew, never make it back to Virginia City in time, never have the slightest chance to save Jimmy Lee Cranston's life. So he walked his mount, letting the animal blow, and letting the sweat dry on its great body.

He had to force himself not to get back in the saddle and start driving the horse again as hard as he had been doing. The terrible sense of time passing prodded him, silently urging him to hurry, to shorten the distance between himself and his goal.

But he continued walking, deliberately putting one foot in front of the other, letting the horse amble along behind him. He wouldn't let himself look up at the sky to see where the sun was in order to learn how much time was slipping away from him.

This is my only chance, he told himself over and over again as he fought the powerful, almost overwhelming, urge to resume his ride. I've got to give him at least a five-mile walkout.

When he estimated that he had covered the distance he had set for himself, he also estimated that he had wasted, in one sense only, an hour, judging by the position of the sun. But he chose to concentrate on the welcome fact that his mount was no longer sobbing but was breathing normally again.

He halted and retrieved the whiskey bottle from his saddlebag. Tilting the dun's head back and prying open its mouth, he poured a generous amount of whiskey down the animal's throat. After returning the bottle to his saddlebag, he stepped into the saddle and resumed his journey.

He was still driving his dun hard, although he had for a second time walked the animal for five miles two hours earlier, when he rode out of the foothills and saw Virginia City just ahead of him.

Through his legs he felt the heaving of his mount's body which told its ominous tale of the animal's rapidly pounding heart and close-to-bursting lungs. Sweat ran down the animal's body. A sweaty froth foamed up from under the saddle flaps. A white-as-snow lather bathed the dun's neck. Its mane dripped.

Sutton drew rein and slid, bone tired, out of the saddle, to stand with one hand gripping his saddle horn to help support himself.

"You've got a heart as big as a barn," he whispered to the horse. "I don't know what I would have done without you and that's a fact."

The dun's nostrils fluttered rapidly as it drew quick ragged breaths. Its head dropped.

"If I had a medal, I'd give it to you," Sutton told the dun as he picked up its reins and began to lead his mount across an open stretch of plain toward the city that lay sprawled in the dark at the foot of Mount Davidson.

When he reached it, he left his horse at the livery barn, telling the boy on night duty there to "water and grain him good and don't put him away wet."

Then, almost staggering under the weight of the awful weariness he was feeling, he made his way to the International Hotel, where he told the desk clerk to wake him at six o'clock in the morning. Then he took the elevator to his room, where he fell asleep fully clothed, too exhausted even to undress.

The next morning, after being awakened by the desk clerk, Sutton hurriedly left the hotel. He checked the jail, but it was still locked. He made his way to a restaurant where he ravenously devoured a breakfast of two baked potatoes, a steak, four slices of johnnycake, three scrambled eggs, and nearly a potful of coffee.

After paying his bill, he again checked the jail. Still locked. He made his way to the combination barbershop and bathhouse, where he bathed, had himself shaved, and had his hair trimmed.

He was pacing impatiently in front of the jail when

Sheriff Cobb finally appeared a few minutes before eight o'clock.

"You're back I see," Cobb said as he unlocked the door to the jail. "Did you get done what you set out to do?"

Sutton followed Cobb into the jail. "I did and I didn't."

As Cobb sat down behind his desk and began to toy with a lead paperweight, he gave Sutton a quizzical glance.

"Rutledge is dead," Sutton explained. "Hank Tully is damn near dead. I haven't been able to get my hands on Etta Spode as of yet."

"What happened?"

Sutton gave Cobb an account of everything that had happened since he left Virginia City, concluding with, "So now, Sheriff, you can let Jimmy Lee go."

"Oh, I can, can I?"

"Sure you can. I just told you that Tully admitted to me that it wasn't Jimmy Lee but some jasper he didn't know who killed Grant and who then set it up to look like Jimmy Lee had gone and done it."

The sheriff shook his head.

"What's wrong?"

"I can't let the kid go just because you come waltzing in here and tell me that one of the witnesses to the killing has said the kid didn't do it."

"Why the hell can't you?"

"It wouldn't be legal. The kid was tried and convicted in a court of law and unless and until there's some new evidence that he's innocent—well, things will just have to take their course, I'm afraid."

Sutton said, "Maybe you didn't understand what I said, Sheriff. I said Tully says Jimmy Lee didn't kill

Grant. And yet here you come whistling down the road to tell me you can't stop the hanging of an innocent boy. What more evidence do you want, Sheriff?"

"You should have brought Tully in to testify under oath to what he told you." Cobb tossed the paperweight from his left to his right hand.

Sutton lost control. "Dammit, Sheriff, Tully is next door to dead. There was no way in the world that I could have brought him back with me given the condition he was in. I never would have made it here myself in time to stop you from hanging Jimmy Lee if—"

Sutton fell silent, realizing that, although he had arrived in time to stop the hanging, it now appeared as if his efforts had all been in vain. Rage rose within him but it failed to entirely block out the growing fear he was also feeling.

"I'm sorry, Luke."

"The hell you are, Sheriff!"

"Well, I'm not going to argue that point with you. I'll just say this. My hands are tied."

Sutton muttered a vivid oath.

"I've got a suggestion for you, Luke. You told me that Tully told you Etta Spode left him with the intention of returning here to Virginia City. Why don't you see if you can locate her. Maybe she'll tell the same story as Tully. You've still got some time. Jimmy Lee's not set to hang until noon tomorrow."

"That's too big a risk to take," Sutton responded. "I can't be sure I'll be able to find her before noon tomorrow. I may be a fair-to-middling tracker, but I'm no bloodhound."

"I wish there was something I could do, Luke."

Sutton leaned down, his hands gripping the edge of Cobb's desk. "There is something you can do. You can let Jimmy Lee go. I'll keep him with me. I'll vouch for him."

"I can't do that," Cobb said flatly.

"Well, by God, I can!" Sutton declared and went for his gun.

At the same instant that Sutton's gun cleared leather, Cobb threw the lead paperweight in his hand. It struck Sutton on the wrist, causing him to drop his weapon.

Cobb sprang to his feet, his own gun in his hand and aimed at Sutton. "You're not taking over my jail, Luke," he bellowed. "You're not breaking a prisoner out of my jail either." He paused, his hard eyes on Sutton. "There's only one sure way to deal with somebody like you. A way that will keep you from interfering with the law until it has run its course."

As Cobb, with his gun still trained on Sutton, came around the side of his desk, Sutton, with his hands in the air, asked, "What is it you're fixing to do?"

"I intend to lock you up till the hanging's over and done with."

"You're locking me up?" Sutton asked incredulously. "Sheriff, you can't do that!"

But after picking Sutton's gun up off the floor, Cobb could and did lock Sutton in a cell next to Jimmy Lee's in the rear of the jail.

When Cobb had returned to his office, Sutton met Jimmy Lee's puzzled gaze and said, "I did my best for you, boy. Trouble is my best wasn't good enough."

"I never expected to see you locked up in here, Mr. Sutton," Jimmy Lee said.

"Nor did I expect to see myself locked up in here."

"Did you find Mr. Rutledge or Miss Spode or Mr. Tully?" Jimmy Lee asked hesitantly as if he were afraid to hear a negative answer.

"I found both Rutledge and Tully."

As Jimmy Lee's eyes lit up, Sutton proceeded to tell his fellow prisoner most of what had happened since they had last met.

When he had finished, Jimmy Lee was beaming. "Then I won't have to hang after all," he crowed happily and did a little dance in the middle of his cell. "I mean now that Mr. Tully has told you the truth the sheriff will have to let me out." When Sutton said nothing, Jimmy Lee, in a strained voice, asked, "He will have to let me out, won't he?"

"I haven't yet told you the end of the story," Sutton said somberly. When he spoke again after a long pause, his voice was bitter. "Sheriff Cobb says he can't let you go unless Tully comes in and swears under oath to the story he told me about the killing of Grant. There was no way I could get him here in time to do that before— before noon tomorrow. I reckon I lost my temper, which is a thing I've been known to do, when I heard that. I went for my gun. I meant to bust you out of here. Then the two of us could have gone hunting Etta Spode. If we couldn't find her, we could always go back to Gideon, get Tully, and haul him back here to speak his piece. But the sheriff got the drop on me and here I am."

"Oh, Lord a'mighty," Jimmy Lee whispered and sank down on his bunk, his expression abruptly grim.

Sutton silently cursed the way things had turned out. After a moment, he spoke again. "How you been bearing up, boy?"

Jimmy Lee, staring dully at the floor, answered, "Well enough, I reckon, all things considered." He looked up at Sutton. "But oh, my Lord a'mighty, I don't know how

I'll do from here on in now that I know I'm done for, for sure."

Sutton gripped the bars that separated his cell from Jimmy Lee's.

"In the days gone by since you come to see me," Jimmy Lee continued, "I had a whole lot of hope. I was thinking you'd get me out of here for sure. But maybe what I was doing wasn't thinking. Maybe it was wishing."

"I'm sorry as hell I let you down, boy."

"Oh, I didn't mean that the way I reckon it sounded, Mr. Sutton," a flustered Jimmy Lee said quickly. "I've just got no way with words. I wasn't slinging mud on you. What I meant was you struck me from the first minute I met you like somebody who no matter what it was they was facing could just take the bull by the horns and get done what needed doing."

Jimmy Lee pounded a fist into the palm of his hand. "There I go again. Talking and not saying nowhere near what I mean."

Sutton took off his hat, went over to his bunk, and lay down upon it to stare blindly up at the ceiling.

"I thank you kindly for all you've done for me, Mr. Sutton," Jimmy Lee said, rising and coming over to the bars that separated him from Sutton. "You run down two out of three. Now, that's real good. What's even better is that you got one of the two to tell you the truth."

"For all the good it did you."

"But you got to admit that some men—maybe most, if you were to ask my opinion—probably wouldn't have been able to track down even one man, let alone two."

Sutton dropped his hat over his face.

"I've met men in my time who couldn't track a belled calf in a corral," Jimmy Lee said.

When Sutton remained silent, Jimmy Lee continued, "Mr. Sutton, I hope this comes out right what I'm going to say. What I'm trying to get at is this. You mustn't go blaming yourself for what happened with the sheriff when you got back here. There weren't no way for you to know that he wouldn't let go of me once you told him what you found out from Mr. Tully. None of that's any fault of yourn, don't you see?"

Well, I'll be damned, Sutton thought. The boy's trying to cheer me up when it's him I should be trying to cheer up.

He removed his hat from his face, sat up, put his hat back on. He looked around the cell and then went up to its one barred window.

"What are you doing, Mr. Sutton?"

Sutton tested the iron bars to see how solidly they were set in place. It took him only seconds to see that they could not be moved. He ran one hand over the heavy planking that formed the walls. He pounded a fist on it. No hollow sound. That wood, he thought, is about as solid as stone. Nobody could bust it down with his bare hands. His eyes fell on his bunk and an idea occurred to him. But he quickly rejected the idea. Even using the bunk as a battering ram wouldn't work. For one thing, the bunk, if used as a battering ram, would make enough noise to wake the dead in Virginia City's Boot Hill. For another, the bunk was too flimsy and would most likely collapse under the assault on the wall.

"Are you looking for a way out of here, Mr. Sutton?"

"I am."

"I spent a fair amount of time in here doing the selfsame thing. I didn't find any."

Sutton pounded a boot heel against the solid puncheon floor. It did not give. He thought of the bowie in his boot. Perhaps he could pry up one of the puncheons. He pulled his knife from his boot and tried to do so in several places—to no avail. The knife blade bent. The puncheons didn't.

He returned his knife to his boot as Jimmy Lee said, "We could maybe think of a way out of here if we had more time, only we don't have much left."

"How come they moved up the date of the hanging?" Sutton inquired as he tested the bars at the front of his cell, which were, he was sorry to find, set firmly in place.

"The hangman, it seems, forgot he had already hired on to hang a pair of horse thieves in Carson City the same day as he took me on," Jimmy Lee answered. "So they moved me up to suit his convenience." Jimmy Lee smiled wanly at Sutton. "They didn't give no thought to my convenience."

"What time do they serve meals in this place?" Sutton asked, his eyes on the narrow space at the base of the cell door through which trays were slid in along the floor to the prisoners.

Jimmy Lee told him.

Maybe, Sutton thought, when the sheriff brings me my dinner I can somehow or other get the jump on him. It's worth a try, he decided and sat down on his bunk to bide his time.

Just after noon, Cobb appeared carrying two covered trays. He set them down on the floor and then drew his gun, which he aimed at Sutton. "Stand back, Luke," he ordered.

Reluctantly, Sutton obeyed the order.

With his foot, Cobb pushed a tray into Sutton's cell and then he repeated the process at the cell next door.

I never got to get near him, Sutton thought, disappointed, as he watched Cobb return to his office. He's too smart to come close to those bars. He no doubt figures I might try some slick scheme. If only there were some way to get him to come up close or open the cell door . . .

He slapped his thigh and a smile appeared on his face. Then the smile faded as his eyes met Jimmy Lee's, which were watching him expectantly. I can go and put my own hide on the line anytime I choose, he thought, but what about the boy? I got no right to drag him in on this plan of mine. Not without his permission, I don't.

He went up to the bars separating the cells and said, "I think I know a way to get us both out of here."

"You do?" Jimmy Lee cried excitedly.

Sutton put a finger to his lips to signal for quiet. "It's a plan that's not without a good deal of risk and not just for me." He outlined for Jimmy Lee the plan for escape that he had just conceived, concluding with, "It's risky like I said, so I won't try it unless you're willing, since your life will be on the line the same as mine will be if things don't work out right."

"Mr. Sutton," Jimmy Lee said softly, "my life is on the line right now as it is. I'm all set to lose it come noon tomorrow. So what you have in mind to do—that's just fine with me. At least it gives me a chance, which the hangman sure won't."

Sutton bent down and retrieved a match from one of the rolled-up cuffs of his jeans. "You're sure you want to go through with this, are you?" he asked Jimmy Lee as he struck the match into fiery red life.

Jimmy Lee nodded with a mixture of eagerness and apprehension, his eyes on the flaming match in Sutton's hand.

Sutton turned and went back to his bunk. Bending down, he touched the blazing match to the bunk's straw-stuffed ticking. He stepped back as the ticking caught fire and flames shot up from it.

He moved to the other side of the cell where the bars separated him from Jimmy Lee and stood there, watching the far wooden wall of his cell catch fire.

"Mr. Sutton, shouldn't we—"

Sutton held up a hand and Jimmy Lee said no more.

When the wall was engulfed in flame, Sutton yelled at the top of his voice, "Fire!"

He expected to see Sheriff Cobb come bursting through the door into the cell area. When the man didn't, he again yelled, *"Fire!"*

The flames spread to the floor and the adjoining wall.

"Cobb!" Sutton yelled as loudly as he could.

No response.

EIGHT

Sutton picked up his metal tray, dumped the food it contained on the floor, and banged it against the bars of his cell while continuing to shout, alternately, *"Fire!"* and *"Cobb!"*

The racket he was making finally roused the sheriff, who came shuffling sleepily through the door into the now smoky cell area. He stopped, stared in wide-eyed disbelief at the flames that were filling almost half of Sutton's cell.

"Get water from the pump at the horse trough outside!" Sutton yelled at him.

Cobb turned and fled.

He was back within minutes with an iron-banded oak bucket full of water. He threw the water through the bars of Sutton's cell.

"That's not going to do it," Sutton shouted at him over the noisy crackling of the flames. "You've got to get water closer to the fire or I'm going to wind up a barbeque."

As Cobb hurriedly left, Jimmy Lee called out, "Mr. Sutton!"

Sutton looked over his shoulder at Jimmy Lee, who was thrusting a horse blanket he had taken from his bunk through the bars at him.

"Mr. Sutton, you could try smothering the fire with this."

Sutton took the blanket from Jimmy Lee, but he did

not use it as the boy had suggested, explaining that he didn't want to put out the fire on his own because that would result in the failure of his escape plan.

Cobb returned with two buckets of water which he hastily set down on the floor. He took his ring of keys from his pocket and fumbled with the lock on the door of Sutton's cell.

"Hurry!" Sutton said, feeling the searing heat and beginning to cough because of the clouds of irritating smoke swirling around him.

Jimmy Lee joined in the coughing as Cobb cursed and then cried, "I can't find the right key!"

But he did find it a moment later and Sutton's cell door, which he unlocked, swung open. Only then did Sutton begin to flail at the flames with the horse blanket Jimmy Lee had given him. Cobb dashed the water from both buckets on the flames, dousing some of them but by no means all of them.

Jimmy Lee called out to Sutton, and when Sutton turned toward him, the boy thrust his lumpy ticking through the bars that separated the cells.

Sutton threw the ticking on the floor to smother the flames that were eating through the puncheons that formed the floor of the cell, successfully smothering them.

Cobb, coughing and wiping his eyes with a polka-dotted handkerchief, sighed as the last of the flames died. "It's a damn good thing you were able to wake me up out of that catnap I was taking," he said. "Usually nothing short of a mine whistle will wake me and then not even that sometimes. What started the fire?"

Before the sheriff could turn around to face Sutton who was standing to one side and behind him, Sutton reached out and pulled the man's gun from its holster.

"What the Sam Hill—" Cobb spluttered, turning around to find his own gun trained on him.

"Sorry for all the fuss, Sheriff," Sutton said insincerely. "But I'm not about to stand by and see the boy swing. Not when he's innocent as a just-born and still-blind pup, I'm not. I'm going to go get Tully and Etta Spode too if I can and bring them back here to straighten this thing out once and for all."

He eased out of his still-smoky cell. He took the ring of keys from the cell door's lock and unlocked Jimmy Lee's cell door.

"Find something to tie the sheriff's hands with," he ordered Jimmy Lee who hurried out of the cell and into the outer office.

"You're going to tie me up?" Cobb asked, his eyes watering and making white marks on his smoke-stained cheeks.

Sutton nodded. Then, when Jimmy Lee returned with a ball of twine, saying it was all he could find, Sutton told him to tie Cobb's hands behind his back. When Jimmy Lee had done so, Sutton tore off an unburned piece of Jimmy Lee's ticking, which he used to gag the sheriff.

"Come on," he said to Jimmy Lee and they both left the cell. Sutton swung its door shut and locked it, and then he dropped the ring of keys on the floor well out of Cobb's reach. He left the cell area, followed by Jimmy Lee.

In the outer office, he proceeded to search the sheriff's desk until he found what he was looking for—his Remington revolver. As he holstered his gun, Jimmy Lee said, "It's been nice knowing you, Mr. Sutton, and I thank you kindly for getting me out of that jail."

"We haven't yet come to the parting of the ways,"

Sutton told him. "You're coming with me. I want to be able to keep an eye on you, make sure the sheriff doesn't catch up with you."

Sutton handed the sheriff's gun to Jimmy Lee, who thrust it into his waistband and asked, "Where are we going, Mr. Sutton?"

"The livery barn."

When they reached it, the farrier gave Sutton a cheerful greeting and then, as he turned to Jimmy Lee, his jaw dropped. "That's—he's the one did in Seth Grant!"

"That's right," Sutton said calmly. "I'm taking him to Carson City where he's to hang tomorrow," he lied.

When the farrier started to say something, Sutton ostentatiously fingered his tin star.

The farrier said, "You'll be wanting your horse."

"I will. My horse and a rental mount for my prisoner here."

The farrier nodded, and Sutton, with his hand on Jimmy Lee's shoulder, went to where his dun was stalled. "That rental horse I'm in need of," he called out to the farrier, "I need him ready to ride."

"Yes, sir, Deputy," the farrier responded. "Always glad to cooperate with the law."

Sutton stuffed the hackamore he had used on the ride back to Virginia City into his saddlebag. He placed on his horse its familiar bridle. By the time he had the dun ready to go, the farrier appeared, leading a black with a white blaze in the middle of its forehead.

Sutton paid what he owed the farrier, and then both he and Jimmy Lee led their mounts out of the livery barn where they stepped into their saddles and rode out of town, heading toward the Sierra Nevada mountains.

When they reached the foothills, Jimmy Lee ventured a question. "Where are we headed, Mr. Sutton?"

"Call me Luke. To answer your question, we're headed to a town in the mountains called Gideon."

"That's where you left Mr. Tully with the doctor, as I recollect."

"You recollect correct. I want to see if Tully's fit enough to travel yet. If he is, we'll bring him back to Virginia City. If he's still too much under the weather to make the trip, we'll leave him with the doc and go looking for Etta Spode."

"Do you know where she is?"

"Nope. Not for sure, I don't. But Tully told me she had headed east after she left him. There's a little town, a sort of mining camp that put down roots and grew, called Silver Dollar, east of where Tully and Etta split up. I figure she might have gone there."

"How come?"

"Well, Tully told me she told him she intended to head back to Virginia City one you'd had your neck stretched and that affair was all over and done with. So I reckon she wouldn't have gone far, since your hanging was only days away from the time she left Tully."

"Mr. Sutton—Luke, I mean—I don't want to mess in matters that you know a lot more about than I do but I'm wondering wouldn't it be better were we to round up both Mr. Tully and Miss Spode. I mean if both of them say I didn't kill Mr. Grant, wouldn't that be twice as good as if just one of them was to say it?"

"You're right on that score, boy. But the way I figure it is, one would be good enough to start off with. That one I hope will turn out to be Tully. It's a case of a bird in the hand being worth two in the bush. If he can travel, we'll take him back to Virginia City and then, unless I miss my guess, Etta Spode will come waltzing back to her parlor house in town as open and above-

board as you please, since she will have figured that by
that time nobody will want to talk to her about Grant's
murder, since as far as she knows, you've already been
hung. Then Sheriff Cobb can pounce on her and see if
she'll tell the same tale about the killing as Tully told
me."

"Do you think she will?"

"Hard to say for sure. But when she finds out what
Tully told me maybe she'll cave in and come clean with
the truth."

"I sure do hope so." Jimmy Lee paused a moment
and then, "Of course, I could run far enough so that
they'd never find me—the law, I mean. That way it
wouldn't matter what anybody said about what I did or
didn't do. I'd be free and no worse for the wear." He
paused again. "But that just don't sit right with me. I
don't want to have to turn tail and run the other way
every time I see some man wearing a badge. What's
more, I'd like to get my good name back."

They made camp that night in a mountain meadow
that was surrounded by tall rounded hummocks and
bordered on the west by a creek.

Sutton skinned and gutted a skunk he had shot back
along the trail, spitted it, and roasted it over a fire
Jimmy Lee had built beneath a towering lodgepole
pine. As he held the carcass over the flames, and fat and
blood dropped from it to sizzle and spit in the fire,
Jimmy Lee returned from the creek where he had gone
to fill Sutton's canteen.

They both drank from it and then they waited in
silence for the skunk to cook. Later, when it was ready,
Sutton cut a piece from it with his bowie, speared the

piece on a stick, and handed the stick to Jimmy Lee who promptly bit into it and as promptly let out a yelp.

"Let it cool down some before you have at it," Sutton advised.

"I should have. Had I, I wouldn't have burned my tongue like I just did. But I haven't eaten anything since breakfast and my stomach's wondering is my throat cut."

Later, when all that was left of the skunk was a small pile of bones with bits of gristle attached to some of them, Jimmy Lee took another drink from Sutton's canteen, handed it to Sutton, wiped his greasy lips and said, "While I was cooling my heels in jail I had a lot of time to think and you know what one of the things was I thought, Luke?"

Sutton gave him a questioning glance and Jimmy Lee continued, "I thought all the time of how I was going to die for something I didn't do and how that wasn't the least little bit fair. There were times—mostly at night when I'd wake up and think it was all a bad dream—that it couldn't really happen to me. But then I'd get my wits about me and I'd know it weren't no dream and I really was going to die.

"I'd get so scared I'd turn cold all over and start in to shiver. Then a funny thing would happen. I'd get mad. I'd get mad at folk for claiming I'd killed Mr. Grant when I knew damn well I didn't.

"All that thinking, it led me to one conclusion and the conclusion I come to, Luke, was that folk just wasn't to be trusted. But then I'd remember you."

It seemed to Sutton that Jimmy Lee was blushing. But, he speculated, maybe it's just the light of the fire on his face.

"I'd remember," Jimmy Lee went on, "how you come

to see me and said you'd do your best to help me out of the bad spot I'd got myself into. That would sort of cancel out all the bad thoughts I'd had about other folk.

"But then a week went by and there weren't a single sign of you, so I went back to thinking nobody was fit to be trusted in this evil old world of ours, you included. But then you come back to try to keep me off the gallows and when it looked like you couldn't do that you turned around and busted us both out of jail. That made me realize something."

"Oh? What was the something it made you realize?"

"That not every apple in the barrel is bad."

"I told you, boy, that your lawyer offered me a fee if I'd lend you a hand."

Jimmy Lee nodded. "I know. But Sheriff Cobb and me was talking one day while you was gone and he told me something too."

"What did he tell you?"

"About how you was once in the same spot a few years back that I was in. He said he read all about you in the newspaper. About how four men bushwhacked your brother and you was tried and convicted of the killing but you got away and hunted down those four men and cleared your name.

"I don't think you're doing what you've been doing for me just for the money, though I wouldn't blame you one bit if you was. A man's got to earn a living one way or the other. But I got to thinking that maybe you saw a little bit of yourself in me, seeing that I was in the same leaking boat you was once in your own self."

"You may be right, boy. I recollect as clear as a bell how it feels to be cornered with what seems like all the people in the world moving in on you with killing on their minds. It's enough to make a man's blood run cold and his hair to all fall out."

"Lord a'mighty," Jimmy Lee exclaimed, "don't I know that to be the truth!"

"We had best get ourselves some sleep," Sutton suggested and got up to get his bedroll. "You can use my blanket, boy. I've got a tarp which will do for me."

Later, as Sutton lay with his unholstered gun near his right hand, Jimmy Lee, not far away from him, turned in his direction and asked, "You asleep yet, Luke?"

"Nope."

"I told you before that I did a lot of thinking while I was in jail but there was one thing I forgot to tell you I thought, which was that one good apple is sometimes enough to make up for a whole bunch of bad ones."

As dawn turned the eastern sky russet, Sutton and Jimmy Lee continued their journey. They found some watercress which nearly completely covered the surface of a stream that crossed their trail and breakfasted on it.

The sky was blue and the sun was well above the horizon when Sutton spotted a rider barely visible in the distance behind him. He rode on, glancing over his shoulder from time to time. The rider—he couldn't tell if it was a man or a woman—continued riding his backtrail.

"We turn here, boy," he said and began to ride at a right angle to the trail he had been following.

"What's wrong, Luke?" Jimmy Lee asked, studying the grim expression on Sutton's face.

"Maybe nothing. But there's a rider behind us. He's been sticking with us for a while now and I don't like it. I want to see if he turns the same as we just did."

Twenty minutes later, from where he lay with his

head just above the crest of a hummock, Sutton had his answer. The rider had also changed direction and was heading toward the hummock.

Sutton went scrambling down the rise, boarded his dun, and rode out with Jimmy Lee, who had been waiting aboard his black for him, following along.

"Did you see anybody, Luke?"

"It's a man and it looks to me like he's trailing us."

"Do you know him?"

Sutton shook his head. "But I don't like somebody breathing down my neck like he's been doing—or seems to have been doing. I admit I don't know for certain that he's trailing us but it sure does look that way. We're going to give him the slip."

For the next hour, Sutton and Jimmy Lee laid down a false trail for the man Sutton had seen following them. Then, backtrailing carefully to leave as little trace of their passage as possible, they resumed their journey and by mid-afternoon they had reached Gideon.

"I'm itching to meet up with Mr. Tully again," Jimmy Lee told Sutton as they rode down the town's main street. "I want to ask him why he knuckled under to the jasper that killed Mr. Grant and didn't stay in town and tell the truth about what happened."

"I can tell you why he didn't."

"He told you?"

"Nope. He didn't tell me but then he didn't have to, not in so many words I mean. He did it because he was scared he'd be killed if he didn't go along. It's that simple—and that complex too."

"I wouldn't have been scared. I would have told the truth."

"Maybe so."

"You think I wouldn't't've?"

"I think when a fellow is sixteen years old he thinks he's not never going to die. That he's going to live forever is what he thinks when he's just sixteen. But a fellow that, say, gets to be around thirty, which is what I take Tully for—then the picture changes some. A fellow of that age, he's found out he's going to die one day and just knowing that sad fact makes him love living, even if his life's a miserable one by most standards."

They drew reins in front of Dr. McDevitt's house. They left their mounts in front of the house and Sutton knocked on the door.

It was opened by Dr. McDevitt, who greeted Sutton with "Oh, it's you. Come in."

Once inside the house, Sutton said, "I didn't have time to tell you the whole story about why I wanted Tully so bad when I was here before, Doc. This here's Jimmy Lee Cranston. He was in jail and waiting to hang for a killing Tully told me the boy didn't do. I'd tracked down another man who witnessed the crime but he was killed before he could tell me what he saw. I've still got a woman name of Etta Spode I'm looking for who also saw the murder, and I'm hoping I can get her to tell the truth and clear the boy's name.

"I tried to get Jimmy Lee out of jail back in Virginia City on the strength of what Tully told me but the sheriff there wouldn't turn him loose. So I busted him out and the two of us, we rode back here to collect Tully and take him back to Virginia City with us to clear the boy's name if he can travel."

"Deputy, I'm afraid I've got bad news for you—if you'll let me get a word in edgewise. Tully's dead."

"Oh, my Lord a'mighty!" Jimmy Lee cried.

Dr. McDevitt said, "Tully passed away only hours after you left here, Deputy. I sent word to that effect to the sheriff in Virginia City by a man who was on his way there. But I suppose you must have left town before he got there."

"How much do I owe you, Doc?" a glum Sutton asked.

Dr. McDevitt shook his head. "The twenty dollars you paid me when you were here before paid for what I and the local mortician did for Mr. Tully. The two of us split the fee. I'm sorry for the way things worked out. I did my best for Tully but he had two punctured lungs."

"Thanks, Doc, I know you did. Well, we'll be on our way."

As Sutton and Jimmy Lee left the house, Dr. McDevitt, in the doorway, called out, "I wish you the best of luck in your search for Etta Spode, Deputy."

Sutton nodded his acknowledgment of the doctor's good wishes.

"What if we can't find her, Luke?" Jimmy Lee asked, his voice shaky.

"We'll find her," Sutton stated with far more certainty than he felt. "We've lost two, but you know what folks say. The third time's the charm." He gave Jimmy Lee a reassuring pat on the back before they both climbed into their saddles and rode out of town.

From Gideon, they headed for the mining town of Silver Dollar. Sutton still felt the same sense of urgency about his quest as he had from the beginning, despite the fact that there was far less danger now of Jimmy Lee dying at the end of a thick hemp rope. But there was always the possibility that Sheriff Cobb had formed a posse to hunt them down. So far he had seen no sign of one.

Now his sense of urgency arose more from the fact that there was somebody somewhere who was also

searching for Etta Spode just as he was but for a more
sinister purpose. That somebody was the man who had
killed Grant and later Rutledge, and finally Tully. The
same man who had vowed, according to Tully, to kill
Etta as well. Sutton found himself still sitting uneasy in
his saddle but he tried to hide his uneasiness from
Jimmy Lee.

Who, he asked himself as he rode along with Jimmy
Lee beside him, was the man who had killed Grant?
What was his motive for killing Grant? He could understand the motive for killing the three witnesses to the
crime. The killer had, according to Tully, regretted the
fact that he had not killed all three witnesses immediately following his murder of Grant. Now he wanted
none of them left alive for obvious reasons.

It was getting dark when they arrived in Silver Dollar.
Like some night-crawling creature, the town was beginning to come to raucous life. From a saloon came the
sound of a hurdy gurdy that was almost drowned out by
shouts and cracked laughter. Men streamed in and out
of another saloon situated farther down the street. A
drunken man reeled from pillar to supporting pillar
beneath the overhang in front of the town's claims and
assay office.

"I don't see any women," Jimmy Lee said. "Maybe
Miss Spode's not here."

"The fact that you don't see any women is the best
reason in the world to think she might be here," Sutton
remarked, scanning the street ahead of him. "There
must be a lot of lonely miners in Silver Dollar, and Etta
Spode is the kind of woman, as you and me know, who
can chase away a man's loneliness—for a price. Maybe
she's busy plying her trade."

When they reached the end of the main street where

respectable frame houses stood clustered together as if for protection from the brawling and boisterous center of town, Sutton turned his dun and headed back the way they had come.

"We'll check the saloons," he told Jimmy Lee. "Ask a few questions."

They left their mounts tied to a hitchrail in front of the first saloon they came to and went inside. Tobacco smoke swirled in the dimly lighted room which was crowded with men.

"She's not here," Jimmy Lee observed dolefully.

Sutton pushed through the crowd and when he reached the bar he ordered whiskey. "What about you?" he asked Jimmy Lee.

"Whiskey."

The bar dog placed a bottle and two not very clean glasses in front of them.

Sutton filled the two glasses and then drank from his. Jimmy Lee drank, grimaced, but managed to keep the rotgut down.

"I'm looking for a woman," Sutton informed the bar dog.

"You and just about every other man in town," the bar dog responded. "You'll have to stand in line to get to the kind of woman I reckon you're looking for. That's because we've only got one. The last one we had —Missy Slade—she died of the clap and that was way last winter. So the boys in town have had a long-lasting itch with no way to scratch it till Kit came to town a little while ago."

Sutton said, "The particular woman I'm looking for ever since I first ran into her in Gold Hill, Nevada, has kind of frizzy yellow hair and blue eyes. Her skin's real smooth."

"That sounds like Kit," the bar dog declared. "She sure does fit the description you just gave of the woman you're looking for."

Sutton put a hand on Jimmy Lee's shoulder to calm the boy, who had begun to fidget.

"You'd better watch your step with Kit though," the bar dog advised. "She packs a two-shot derringer and she knows how to use it. She shot and wounded the circuit preacher when he came by here last night, and she did it, she said, because he kept biting her all during their prayer meeting." Sly laughter.

"Where can I find this Kit?" Sutton inquired.

"She rents a room in the hotel down the street."

Sutton emptied his glass and pointed to Jimmy Lee's.

"I've had enough," the boy said and then followed Sutton outside and down the street to the hotel.

In the lobby, where a number of men were gathered at a small bar at one end of the room, Sutton asked the desk clerk for the room number of "Miss Kit."

The acne-scarred clerk gave Sutton a leer. "Number two," he said. "Up those steps over there, turn right."

Moments later, Sutton was knocking on the door of room number two.

"Who is it?" a bored female voice called out from behind the closed door.

"That's her!" Jimmy Lee exclaimed.

Sutton silenced him with a gesture. "Open up, Kit," Sutton called out. "I've got me two pockets full of coin I'm itching to empty."

The door opened.

When Etta Spode, a shocked and alarmed expression on her face, tried to slam it shut, Sutton put a boot between the door and the jamb, preventing her from doing so.

Then, when she noticed Jimmy Lee standing off to one side, one hand flew up to cover her mouth and she pointed a finger at him. "You!" was all she managed to say.

"Good evening, Miss Spode," Jimmy Lee said stonily.

Sutton pushed the door wide open. As he did so, Etta backed into the lamp-lighted room, saying, "They hanged you!" to Jimmy Lee and then, "You're dead!"

"You can see as plain as day I'm not," Jimmy Lee said as he followed Sutton into the room and closed the door behind him.

"What—how—" Etta spluttered nervously, apparently unable to take her eyes off Jimmy Lee.

"Luke here," Jimmy Lee said, "busted me—both of us—out of jail and we come stalking you, Miss Spode."

"Which was an easy enough thing to do," Sutton commented laconically, "even though you do have more names than a cat has lives. Kit, Dolly—"

"What do you want?" Etta asked, finally shifting her haunted gaze from Jimmy Lee to Sutton.

"You know the answer to that question," he told her. "I'm here for the same reason I tracked you down that other time when Tully was with you. Namely, to take you back to Virginia City and let the law ask you a few questions about the night Seth Grant was shot to death."

"Miss Spode," Jimmy Lee began, "how come you didn't stay and tell the sheriff the truth about what happened that night?"

Etta lowered her eyes. She looked everywhere but at Jimmy Lee.

Sutton said, "Hank Tully told me it was a man he

didn't know who stormed into your place and shot Grant to death."

An obviously flustered Etta began to vigorously, almost frantically, shake her head. Her lips parted, but she seemed to be unable to speak.

"Who was that man?" Sutton asked her. "Why did he kill Grant?"

Still shaking her head like a mechanical doll, Etta answered, "There was no other man. If Tully told you that, he was lying. He was just making up stories—totally untrue stories."

"Why would he lie?" Sutton probed.

"How should I know?"

"Why are *you* lying?" Sutton asked. "Is it on account of you're scared to death of whoever killed Grant and who's also killed Rutledge and Tully?"

Etta gasped. "Hank Tully has been killed too?"

Sutton nodded and said, "Tully didn't die right away. He'd been stabbed in the back and left for dead. He said the man who did it was the same one who had killed Rutledge earlier. He told me that man said he was going out after you, Etta, and, when he caught up with you, he was going to kill you too. Now, I wonder what you have to say about that."

Etta had nothing to say. Her face blanched. Fear flared in her eyes.

"I can see that news doesn't make you any too happy," Sutton observed. "Which I can well understand. I wouldn't be too happy either knowing a bushwhacker was traveling my backtrail."

Etta sat down on the bed. "I've got to get away," she murmured.

"You are going to get away," Sutton assured her.

"You're going back to Virginia City with me and Jimmy Lee like I already told you."

"No. I don't dare." Etta glanced at Sutton. "Don't you see that I can't? If what you have told me is true—"

"Oh, it's true all right."

"—then I have no choice but to run—to get to a place that's safe."

"And leave me to run from the law for the rest of my natural life?" Jimmy Lee interjected angrily. "Ain't you gone and done enough harm to me as it is, Miss Spode, you and those two men? Don't you think it's high time you started in on making amends for what you've done to me?"

"Oh, Jimmy Lee," Etta suddenly cried, tears brimming in her eyes as she fumbled nervously with her skirt. "I never wanted to do you harm."

"Then why did you?" Jimmy Lee persisted.

When Etta made no reply, Sutton said, "Tully told me the man who stabbed him and shot Rutledge to death told him that he had threatened to kill Rutledge's wife if he told the truth about Grant's murder. What did that killer threaten you with, Etta?"

"Nothing."

"He didn't threaten to kill you if you told the truth?"

"No!"

"Then why did you run?"

Instead of answering Sutton's question, Etta pulled up her skirt. A derringer that had been strapped to her leg by her garter appeared in her hand and pointed directly at Sutton's gut.

NINE

"Don't move, either of you!" Etta ordered, the derringer in her hand steady, her eyes flickering between Sutton and Jimmy Lee.

"Miss Spode—" Jimmy Lee began but was immediately silenced by Etta's, "I'm getting out of here and if either one of you try to follow me, I'll put holes in your hide."

She edged around the room, keeping Sutton and Jimmy Lee well away from her as she moved toward the door.

"Luke," Jimmy Lee whispered, "we got to stop her."

Sutton was thinking the same thing. But he didn't want to get shot, and he thought the nervousness brightening Etta's eyes might lead to that very thing if he tried to rush her and wrest the gun from her hand. He could go for his own gun—but he didn't want to shoot—and possibly kill—Etta. So he stood his ground, waiting for any opening that might present itself, prepared to make his move if the moment ever came.

It didn't.

Etta was out the door and slamming it shut behind her.

As Jimmy Lee lunged for the door, Sutton put a hand on the boy's shoulder to restrain him.

A key turned in the door's lock.

"Why didn't you let me go after her?" Jimmy Lee cried.

"I didn't want you shot, that's why," Sutton answered, going to the door and listening at it.

"Now what are we going to do, Luke?"

Sutton crossed the room and looked out the window. There was a long drop from it to the ground below. A man might make it were he to jump, he thought. He also might wind up with a busted leg or two if he tried going that route. He went back to the door and, putting his shoulder against it, heaved. The solid door didn't budge.

"Stand back," he said to Jimmy Lee. When the boy had moved to one side, Sutton drew his revolver and fired at the lock.

It splintered, sending wooden chips and iron fragments flying through the air in every direction.

Sutton reached out, opened the door, and told Jimmy Lee to stay behind him.

When Jimmy Lee drew his gun, Sutton said, "Don't shoot her whatever you do. She's no good to you dead."

He stepped out into the hall and, finding it empty, made his way to the stairs. He had just started down them, with Jimmy Lee right behind him, when he saw the men who had been drinking at the bar when he arrived at the hotel gathered at the foot of the stairs, the desk clerk among them.

All of them were staring up at him and at Jimmy Lee. All but one of them had a gun in his hand. The one without a gun, a burly man wearing a checkered shirt and twill trousers he seemed about to burst out of, had a club in his hands.

Sutton halted and Jimmy Lee bumped into him. He raised his hands, the gun still in his right hand, and then Jimmy Lee, seeing the men below, did the same.

"What for are they fixing to shoot us, Luke?" the boy whispered.

"Miss Kit is a friend of ours," drawled a gaunt man with a waxed mustache, as if he were answering Jimmy Lee's question, which he could not have heard. "What's more, she's new in town," the man continued. "Now us gents here in Silver Dollar are a neighborly bunch. We like to make folks welcome in our town. We made Miss Kit feel real welcome right from the time she first set foot in town, didn't we boys?"

There was a cheer, several whistles, some bawdy laughter.

But the gaunt man, who appeared to be the spokesman for the crowd which, Sutton knew, might at any minute become a mob, did not cheer, laugh, or whistle —or even so much as smile.

"Miss Kit just told us that you were trying to make trouble for her," he continued. "She didn't tell us why and we didn't ask her to tell us why. What we did do is put her where you won't be able to lay a hand on her, lawman."

"She was a witness to a murder," Sutton told the crowd. "This boy behind me was going to hang for that murder which he didn't commit. I meant to get the lady you call Miss Kit to tell the law back in Virginia City who really committed the crime. I plan to take her back to Virginia City where the murder took place—"

"Over my dead body," said the man with the waxed mustache.

There was an ominous chorus of "Over mine too's."

Sutton decided to try a different tack. "We don't mean for any harm to come to her. Like I just said, I plan to take her to—"

"You're not taking Miss Kit anywhere," the crowd's

spokesman stated bluntly. "If you did that she might take a fancy to the fast ways of a wicked place like Virginia City, and we might never get to see her again. Now, that would be a crying shame, that would."

"I hope you boys know that what you're doing is you're obstructing justice," Sutton said and took a step closer to the men gathered at the foot of the stairs.

His remark was met with hoots of mocking laughter.

"What you were doing, lawman," yelled a man from the midst of the crowd, "was obstructing us in our pursuit of pleasure with Miss Kit, if you take my meaning, and we just can't let you go and do that."

"All right," Sutton said and descended one more step. "You boys win. I've got no high card left to play in this game. So if you'll just let me and the boy by we'll go get our horses and ride out."

"That sounds like a good idea, don't it, Harry?" one of the men asked the man with the mustache.

Harry nodded and said, "We don't want to have to shoot you, lawman. But we do want to convince you and your friend that neither one of you is welcome in Silver Dollar. Boys, let's set the tar to boiling. Ames, you go get the feathers."

As two men detached themselves from the crowd and left the hotel, Harry barked, "Throw your guns down here, you two!"

"Luke?" Jimmy Lee said.

"Do like he says, boy," Sutton said.

When Sutton had obeyed Harry's order, Jimmy Lee did the same.

Then, as Harry, grinning, bent over to pick up the two guns lying at his feet, Sutton sprang. He seemed to go flying down the remainder of the stairs. He landed on Harry's back, taking the man down to the floor with him. They rolled over, Harry bellowing wordlessly and dropping his club in the process, Sutton struggling to overpower the man. At last, he succeeded in getting his left forearm around Harry's neck. He applied pressure as he got to his feet, dragging Harry up with him. Harry gagged and began to tear at Sutton's arm that was choking him.

The men in the crowd hesitated briefly and then began moving in on Sutton and his captive. As they did so, Sutton's knees bent. Taking Harry down with him, he retrieved Jimmy Lee's gun and yelled, "Catch!"

After tossing the gun to Jimmy Lee, Sutton picked up his Remington and rammed its muzzle against Harry's right temple. His action stopped the advancing men in their tracks.

"I'll kill him if any of you boys try to take me," Sutton muttered through clenched teeth. "And my partner up there on the stairs, he'll drill at least one and maybe more of you. So I don't think you should do anything foolish unless you want your ringleader here to die and for maybe some of you to suffer the same unnecessary fate."

Sutton spotted the desk clerk slinking through the crowd, the gun in his hand hidden by the men directly in front of him. Just as Sutton was about to twist to the side to place Harry between himself and the desk clerk who was obviously about to make a move, a shot roared in the otherwise silent lobby and the desk clerk let out a yelp, dropped his gun, and ran out the front door.

"Good going!" Sutton called out to Jimmy Lee without turning around.

"I didn't hit him, Luke," Jimmy Lee called back. "That was just a warning shot I sent over his head."

"Let that be a lesson to the rest of you," Sutton said,

addressing the now cowed crowd in front of him. "You heard my partner say he wasn't trying to shoot that jasper. If he had been, he would have, believe me. Why, I've seen him shoot the wings off a fly at fifty paces." He grinned at the sound of Jimmy Lee's guffaw that his lie had elicited.

"Let go of me!" Harry pleaded in a choked voice. "I can't breathe."

Sutton tightened his grip on the man's neck.

Harry gagged and clawed helplessly at Sutton's iron-sinewed forearm that was like a crowbar pressing against his windpipe.

"Where is she?" Sutton asked the men in the crowd. "You tell me where I can find the woman and I'll let Harry here live."

Silence.

The men looked at one another somewhat shame-facedly and then away, avoiding Sutton's eyes.

"Jimmy Lee," Sutton said in a silken voice that was slippery with menace, "what say you shoot that big fellow in the checkered shirt and twill trousers first?"

"That's fine with me, Luke. He's such a big one I'm sure I wouldn't miss him were I to take aim at him blindfolded."

The man Jimmy Lee took aim at tried to sidle in among the others in the crowd but they hurriedly pushed him away so that he was standing alone again.

He raised the gun in his hand and took aim at Jimmy Lee.

Sutton's gun left Harry's temple, roared, and the gun in the hand of the man who had taken aim at Jimmy Lee went spinning into the air before falling to the floor.

"Leave it be or you're dead," Sutton warned him.

He left it there.

"I'm going to ask you all one more time," Sutton said, his eyes roving from face to face in front of him. "And you're going to answer me this time or Harry gets it. Where's the woman?"

It was Harry who answered as Sutton had fully expected it would be. "The livery," he gasped. "The loft in the livery."

Sutton kept his gun pressed against Harry's head as he shoved his prisoner toward the crowd, which parted to let the two men pass.

"Wait!" Harry cried as Jimmy Lee ran down the steps and took up a position beside Sutton. "You said you'd let me go if we told you where she was."

"You got that all wrong, Harry," Sutton said, backing slowly and cautiously now toward the lobby's front door. "I never said no such thing, did I, Jimmy Lee?"

"No, sir, you didn't."

"What are you going to do with me?" Harry asked fearfully, spittle flying from between his lips.

At the door, Sutton said, "You boys heard Harry's question, I reckon. Well, this is my answer. I'm taking Harry over to the livery while my partner and me round up the lady. Now why, you may wonder, would I want to do a thing like that? The answer's easy. To keep any of you hotheads from doing anything rash. Like trying to come after us. If I see so much as even one of your whiskers, Harry's going to leave the living and leave as fast as spit on a hot stove. You boys—have you all got that?"

The men nodded sullenly.

"For good measure and to make sure you're not tempted to do anything foolish, my partner will take your guns. You can collect them and your friend, Harry, at the livery once him and me and the woman have left town. Go get them, Jimmy Lee."

When Jimmy Lee had his arms full of six-guns, he and Sutton, who was still holding Harry prisoner, left the hotel and began backing away toward the livery in case any of the men they had left behind in the hotel lobby decided to come after them despite Sutton's warning.

None did, although most of them gathered just outside the hotel where they were joined by the man named Ames, who returned carrying a gunnysack from which, through a hole in it, white chicken feathers fluttered to the ground.

When Sutton reached the square of lamplight that flooded from the open door of the livery, he released his hold on Harry and shoved the man away from him.

"Don't run!" he commanded. "Stand right there and listen to me." He proceeded to explain to Harry what he wanted done.

When he had finished, Harry swallowed hard, rubbed his throat gingerly with one hand, and said, "You want me to go in there and tell Miss Kit you're hot on her trail."

Sutton nodded.

"You want me to tell her she's got to come down out of the loft and go away with me."

"You got it, Harry. I want you to bring her on out here, and then I want you to get out of the way fast. I don't know if you know it or not but the lady's toting a derringer. There might be some shooting. You don't want to get caught in the middle of it, so step lively and leave the lady to me. If you try tricking me, I'll shoot you for sure. That's a promise."

As Harry entered the livery barn, Sutton instructed Jimmy Lee to pile the weapons he had taken from the

men in the hotel on the far side of the building, which
the boy promptly did. When he returned, Sutton indicated that he was to take up a position on the side of the
livery's open door directly opposite Sutton's own position.

"When Harry comes out with her," Sutton told
Jimmy Lee in a muted voice, "you make sure he steers
clear of the action. I'll go after Etta."

"Be careful, Luke. She might use her gun."

"She might. But I'm counting on the fact that she
won't be suspecting anything—not with her friend
Harry by her side."

At the sound of two men's voices drifting out into the
night from the livery, Sutton gestured Jimmy Lee into
silence. They waited, both of them with their guns in
their hands and their backs pressed against the side of
the building on opposite sides of the door.

That's Harry's voice, Sutton thought as he recognized the sound of the man's voice. That other one
must be the farrier's. Their voices were quickly joined
by a third—Etta's.

Sutton heard the scrape of shoe leather and guessed
it was the sound of Etta descending the ladder from the
loft. He caught an occasional word from an exchange
between Harry and Etta: "lawman," "on the scout for
you."

Moments later, Harry, with Etta by his side, emerged
from the barn, appearing first as silhouettes with the
lamplight behind them, and then as shadowy figures in
the light that leaked from the livery.

When Harry suddenly darted to one side, Sutton
stepped out of the darkness, his gun in his hand.

When Etta saw him, she gave an aborted cry and
reached for the hem of her skirt. He grabbed her arm.

She jerked away from him, started to run, still fumbling with her skirt as she sought her derringer.

Jimmy Lee put out a foot and tripped her. She fell to the ground in a frothy flounce of red skirt and white petticoat. Sutton lunged toward her, saw the gun in her hand, leaped adroitly to one side as she fired at him, and then pounced on her before she could fire the remaining shot in her weapon.

She clawed at his face with her free hand while trying to club him with the small gun in her other hand. He warded off her fingernails with his gun hand while simultaneously seizing her wrist and forcing her to drop her derringer. Then he unceremoniously hauled her, cursing and still clawing, to her feet.

"Damn you, Harry!" she screeched, twisting and turning violently in her frantic efforts to break free of Sutton. "You handed me over to him! *Why?*"

"We tried, all of us did, to protect you, honey," Harry whined. "You've got to believe me, we truly did."

"You didn't!" Etta accused.

"That lawman and the kid with him, they got the drop on the whole bunch of us," Harry explained. "I had to do what they wanted or they'd have killed me. Honey, I'm sorry."

Etta shouted something at Harry that made Jimmy Lee blush.

"You can skedaddle now, Harry," Sutton told him. "Go back and join your friends at the hotel."

When Harry had gone, Sutton told Jimmy Lee to get their horses from the livery. "Etta's too, if it's in there." As the boy started for the livery's door, Sutton advised, "Watch your step in there. The farrier just might turn out to be another friend of Etta's who might decide to try being her champion."

When Jimmy Lee disappeared inside the livery, Etta suddenly lowered her head and bit Sutton's hand that was still gripping her arm.

He let out a yell but he didn't release her. She tried the maneuver again and this time when she did he slammed her up against the wall of the livery. She didn't try it a third time. They stood in cold silence just beyond the reach of the lamplight until Jimmy Lee returned with Sutton's dun, which he handed over, and then, moments later, with his own black and another horse.

"The farrier said this one's Miss Spode's." Jimmy Lee indicated the third horse.

"I'm going to let go of you," Sutton told Etta. "Don't try to run for it or you and me are going to have at it and I assure you you won't like one bit my lack of gentlemanly manners. Now climb aboard your horse, and let's get out of here before your friends up at the hotel get back their nerve and take a notion to try something foolish for the second time tonight."

Moments later, the three rode out of Silver Dollar with Jimmy Lee remarking to no one in particular, "I sure am glad we got out of there when and the way we did. I don't take kindly to the idea of being tarred and feathered like they was fixing to do to us any more than I do to being hanged."

He gave Etta a glance but she ignored him as she maintained the sullen silence into which she had lapsed.

But she broke that silence some time later with, "I'm dead tired and I don't intend to travel like this all night long."

Sutton, hiding his annoyance with her, said, "We can make camp if that's what you want but I thought we'd keep on till we got to Gideon."

"That's another thing," Etta snarled. "Why are we heading south when Virginia City is east of us? I thought you said you were taking me back to Virginia City."

"I am," Sutton said, "but there are no towns between Silver Dollar and Virginia City and we need some food for the trip ahead of us. Unless you're willing to do without any till we get to where we're going."

Instead of speaking, Etta glared at Sutton.

But later, after they had built a fire and spread their bedrolls at a wooded spot Sutton had chosen, she thawed. Sitting on the ground next to Sutton with a blanket wrapped around her like a shawl, she said, "I suppose I should be grateful to you."

"What for?"

"For protecting me from the man you say is going to try to kill me the same as he killed Rutledge and Hank Tully."

Sutton shrugged.

"Do you think he really will try to kill me?"

Sutton glanced at Etta. Her features appeared tense in the flickering firelight and there had been a shakiness in her voice when she spoke which suggested fear lurking behind her apparent nonchalance. "I've no reason to doubt what Tully told me when I found him."

"You mean the man—whoever he is—is out to kill those of us who saw Jimmy Lee kill Seth Grant."

"I didn't kill him!" exclaimed Jimmy Lee who had been tending the fire. He turned angry eyes on Etta.

"Why don't you stop pretending?" Sutton asked Etta. "You know the man who's hunting you is the one who killed Grant. Why don't you just say so and save everybody a whole peck of trouble?"

"Seth Grant was good to me," Etta mused, looking

into the fire instead of at either Sutton or Jimmy Lee. "He gave me presents." She held out her right hand on which an opal blazed almost as brightly as the campfire. "He gave me this ring. And ever so many other things too. He was going to marry me."

Sutton gave a sceptical snort.

"It's true!" an indignant Etta cried. "He was and he would have—if he hadn't been killed."

"Well," Sutton remarked, "it appears we're making some progress. At least you've got to the point where you say Grant was killed, not that Jimmy Lee killed him."

"I saw what I saw," Etta insisted stubbornly, "and I'm not changing my story for anyone—you included."

Sutton noted the hopeless look that paled Jimmy Lee's face as the boy stared despondently at Etta.

"Take a look at it this way," Sutton suggested to her. "If you and Grant were such good—ah, friends, how come you don't want to see the man who really did kill him pay the price for what he did?"

Etta said nothing.

Sutton noted the way her upper teeth worried her lower lip. He decided to try another approach in the hope of getting Etta to change her story and confirm what Tully had told him—that a man Tully didn't know had murdered Grant. "If you don't give a hoot what happens to the boy," he said, "you ought to give one for yourself."

"What does that mean?"

"That bushwhacker who's already killed two men is determined, the way Tully told it to me, to do the self-same thing to you, who happens to be the last person alive who saw him kill Grant. Now, if you were to tell me who he is—if you know—I could tell Sheriff Cobb when we get back to Virginia City, and he could do his best to put the man behind bars where he belongs. That way, you'd be safe from him."

Etta drew the blanket more tightly about her shoulders but Sutton saw her shiver.

"I don't believe your story," she stated without much conviction.

"About the bushwhacker? Believe it or not, it's a true story."

Etta stared at Sutton for a long moment. Then, looking away, she said, "I'm going to try to get some sleep."

"We'll be on our way early," Sutton warned her as she lay down on the ground and covered herself with the blanket. "I want to get you back to town and put away someplace safe before that bushwhacker has a chance to catch up with you."

When Etta did not respond, Sutton turned to Jimmy Lee and said, "We've got to stand guard. I'll take the first shift and wake you up when it comes your turn."

"You think we might have trouble, Luke?"

"Rutledge did. So did Tully."

But the night passed without incident of any kind except that the flight of a horned owl through the trees startled Jimmy Lee during his watch, causing him to fire at the bird, waking both Sutton, whose hand was on his gun even before his eyes had opened, and Etta who cried, "Oh, what is it? What's wrong?"

Jimmy Lee shamefacedly confessed to what he had done.

Sutton, seeing the boy's embarrassment in the dying light of the campfire, commented, "Better that you got off a shot at what turned out to be only an owl than that you didn't get off a shot and the noise you'd heard was made by that bushwhacker on his way here to have a tête-à-tête with our lady friend."

"Stop that!" Etta cried. "You're just trying to frighten me to make me lie and say Jimmy Lee didn't kill Seth."

Sutton thought it would be futile as well as a waste of time to rebut her accusation.

He remained awake and alert the remainder of the night after he had persuaded Jimmy Lee to get some sleep. He heard nothing that was not a natural part of the night. He saw nothing that gave him cause for alarm.

At the first faint light of false dawn, he roused the others and they were on their way before the dawn broke.

They had been on the trail for some time with the sun up and the air warming, none of them talking, when Etta broke their silence by asking when they could expect to reach Gideon.

"By day's end for sure," Sutton replied. "Why do you ask? You in a hurry to get there?"

"Of course I'm in a hurry to get there. I'm starving to death."

They had gone less than another mile when Sutton suddenly drew rein and directed his companions to do the same.

"What are we stopping here for?" Etta complained. "If we keep going we'll reach Gideon that much sooner —and be able to get something to eat there."

"You should have thought of that last night," Sutton told her. "You remember I wasn't the one in favor of stopping. But never mind about that now." He dismounted and pulled up some plants which resembled dandelions except for the fact that they grew nearly four feet tall. He offered one to Etta and one to Jimmy Lee.

"What's this?" Etta asked, staring at the plant Sutton had given her.

"Chicory," he answered. "The young leaves make good eating."

Etta stared at him as if he had lost his mind. "Chicory is for making coffee with, not for eating raw."

"You're right and you're wrong," Sutton told her. "Sure, you can make coffee with chicory. My ma used to. She also used to candy the flower petals and that was a real delicacy I can tell you. But you can also eat the young leaves, like I said. The old ones tend to be bitter. Try some."

Etta made an expression of distaste but then she tore off a leaf and put it in her mouth.

"They're good, Luke," Jimmy Lee said after stuffing several of the leaves into his mouth and chewing on them.

"I'm thirsty," Etta complained as she continued to eat the smallest leaves of the chicory plant in her hand.

Sutton took his canteen down from his saddle horn and shook it. "Empty," he said. "There's a crick over there. See it?"

Etta looked in the direction he was pointing and then started for the creek, the surface of which glowed golden in the bright light of the rising sun.

"Hold on," Sutton called out to her. "The three of us will go together. I don't want you to try running off on me again."

Ignoring the look of disgust Etta gave him, he began to lead his dun in the direction of the creek. Etta and Jimmy Lee rode beside him, Jimmy Lee on his left, Etta on his right.

They had almost reached the creek when Sutton suddenly halted and said, "Dismount, you two!"

"What is it?" Etta cried in alarm as he manhandled her out of the saddle and down to the ground to stand beside him. "Down, boy!" he ordered Jimmy Lee.

"What is it?" Etta cried a second time as Jimmy Lee slid down to the ground between his and Sutton's horses.

"Somebody's up there on that rise," Sutton answered. "I saw the sun shining on a gun barrel."

"Is it the jasper who was trailing us before, Luke?" Jimmy Lee asked.

Sutton's answer was drowned out as a round from a carbine *pinged* through the air toward them.

TEN

"Take cover!" Sutton yelled.

"Where?" Etta cried, looking around her.

"Over there," he said, pointing. "Wait!" he yelled as Etta started to make a run for it. "Grab hold of your stirrup and lead your horse to that grove of trees over there," he ordered her. "You do the same, boy," he told Jimmy Lee. "Keep your horses between you and whoever's on the rise. Better your mounts get shot than you do. Now move!"

As Etta and Jimmy Lee obeyed his orders, Sutton pulled his Winchester from its saddle boot. Taking aim over the rump of his dun, he squeezed off a shot just moments after the gunman on the rise had fired his carbine several times in quick succession. Sutton's shot missed its target but caused the gunman to drop down out of sight.

My bet is he was aiming at Etta, Sutton thought. It's not likely he was out to kill Jimmy Lee. He sure wasn't shooting my way. A thrill coursed through him, setting his heart to beating faster and making his blood begin to drum in his ears. It's him, he thought as he waited to see if the gunman would reappear. It's the man, I'll wager a lifetime's wages, who killed Grant, Rutledge, and Tully. Now he's after Etta to make a clean sweep of things. Is it the jasper who was trailing me and the boy, he asked himself. He didn't know because the man was too far away to identify.

Sutton grabbed a handful of his mount's mane. Tugging hard on it, he led the dun toward the trees into which Etta and Jimmy Lee had disappeared, keeping the horse's body between him and the gunman on the rise.

When he reached the trees, he moved in under the green canopy of their branches and rejoined his companions in a sun-dappled glade.

"Did you get him, Luke?" Jimmy Lee asked eagerly.

"Missed him." Sutton handed his rifle to Jimmy Lee. "Use this if he tries coming down here. Keep a sharp lookout. At the first sign of him, you use this rifle to keep him far away from you."

"What are you going to do?" Etta asked.

"Go get him," was Sutton's curt reply.

As Sutton swung into the saddle, Etta said, "It's him, isn't it? It's the man who killed Rutledge and Hank."

"Can't say for sure," Sutton told her. "But if I had to hazard a guess I think a safe one would be to say that he was shooting at you and that, I reckon, makes him the man who killed Grant, Tully, and Rutledge."

Etta, wringing her hands, pleaded, "Don't leave us."

"It's all right, Miss Spode," Jimmy Lee said softly. "I'll stand by you. For that gunman to get to you, well, he'll have to do it over my dead body."

Sutton impaled Etta with his eyes. "What do you have to say to that?"

"I say no mere boy can protect me from that gunman out there," Etta replied.

"That's not what I meant by my question," Sutton said. "I meant what do you say about the fact that the boy you were willing to let hang when you could have saved him by telling the truth is now ready to put his life on the line to save yours if it should come down to that? How does that make you feel?"

For a moment, Etta was silent. Then, in a hushed tone of voice, she answered with a single word: "Awful."

Sutton turned his dun and rode away.

He made his way through the trees until he was sure he would not be seen by the gunman on the rise—if he was still up there—when he emerged from them. Once out of the grove, he circled around until he was behind the rise. Then he rode back the way he had come, paralleling his earlier course through the trees, keeping the rise on his left. When he was halfway to the spot where he had seen the gunman, he drew his revolver, dismounted, and made his way forward on foot.

He moved cautiously, surveying the terrain ahead and on both sides of him with a steady back and forth sweep of his eyes as he searched for the bushwhacker. He slowed his pace as he approached the spot where he thought the man should be if he had remained where he was previously. There was no one there. Sutton moved closer and then began to climb the rise. At its crest, he saw the bent and broken blades of grass where the man had been. Studying the ground, he soon found the man's trail, which was revealed to him by the mark of a broken boot heel in a bare patch of ground and by a branch broken from a bush which lay on the ground secreting sap, indicating that it had only recently been severed.

He continued following the man's trail, his thumb on the cocked hammer of his gun, his eyes narrowed to keep them from being blinded by the bright sun. He made his way down the rise where the trail abruptly turned. Ahead of him was a deep gorge. As he entered it minutes later, he heard a horse nicker a split second before he saw the horse itself—and the man with his foot in a stirrup as he prepared to climb aboard the animal.

At the same instant, as if he had sensed the presence of another person nearby, the man turned, saw Sutton, swung swiftly into the saddle, and galloped away.

Sutton yelled to him to stop. When he didn't but instead slammed spurs into his horse's flanks to increase its speed, Sutton raised his gun, aimed, and fired at the fleeing man he had recognized as the same one who had been trailing him and Jimmy Lee earlier.

His warning shot did not slow the man down. Sutton swore and then turned and ran as fast as he could back the way he had come, his heart hammering, his breath coming in short shallow gasps.

When he reached his dun, he leaped into the saddle, grabbed the reins, and sent the horse galloping off in the direction the gunman had taken. The light breeze that had been blowing became the sound of a wild wind in his ears as his speed increased. It lifted the hair that covered his ears and the nape of his neck and sent it flying as it did his dun's mane.

Instead of riding down into the gorge when he reached it, he rode the rimrock above it. From his vantage point, he could see the trail of the man he was after—the dug-up ground, the occasional stone that had been struck and chipped by the iron shoe of a horse.

He continued following the trail as fast as he could without losing it. It led out of the gorge and into a valley thick with junipers that slowed his progress somewhat and kept him from seeing clearly what was ahead of him. Doggedly, he rode through the obstacle course confronting him. He was rewarded with a glimpse of his quarry when he crested the mountain on the far side of the valley.

He's a good mile ahead, Sutton estimated, maybe a mile and a half. Kneeing his horse, he went after him.

The man vanished.

What the hell—

Sutton continued on the course he had been traveling, but he was sure he had gone more than a mile and he had seen no trace of the bushwhacker. He drew rein, turned his horse, and looked back the way he had come. His eyes roamed up and down the rolling hills on either side of him and came to rest on a craggy outcropping of rock that jutted up from the ground like a pillar with grassy sides leading up to it.

He headed for it, intending from that vantage point to survey the surrounding area. He had just started up the side of the mesalike formation when a shot sounded behind him. His horse screamed as a round creased its flank, digging a shallow trench in the animal's sleek hide.

As the dun slowed and its gait became erratic, Sutton struggled for control of the animal. After a brief battle, which he won, the dun steadied. Sutton threw one leg over his saddle horn and slid down to the ground where he took cover behind the thick trunk of an aged sycamore. His horse trotted a few more steps and then swung its head around. Its lips drew back over its teeth and it tried to bite the wound on its flank from which blood was now flowing in crimson rivulets.

Sutton waited for what he was sure was coming, wanting it to happen, needing it to happen so that he would know where his assailant was located.

The shot, when it did come, was a relief to him. His eyes fastened on a cleft in a nearby hillside from which the shot had come. He's nearly out of my gun's range, he thought. When he saw movement in the cleft, he fired. Dirt flew from one side of the cleft.

A moment later, when he saw the barrel of his quarry's carbine poke out into the open, he left his cover and ran a few paces to the right. Ignoring the fact that he was out in the open now and an easy target, he gripped his six-gun in both hands and fired.

He smiled in satisfaction as the carbine's barrel was abruptly withdrawn without another shot having been fired from it.

He spun around, raced back to his horse, boarded it, and rode out. Once he had his dun pointed in the direction he wanted to go, he dropped the reins but did not loosen the pressure he was applying to it with his knees. He removed the empty shells from his revolver's chamber and then thumbed fresh cartridges out of his belt which he used to replace them. He picked up his reins with his left hand and then turned his mount and started up the side of the sloping ground that would lead him to the rim of the cleft where the man he was after was holed up.

But as he reached the top of the slope and dismounted, he found that the man was no longer there. He realized at once what had happened when he saw the narrow opening at the rear of the cleft that was just wide enough for a horse and rider to pass through.

He turned his horse and rode down to level ground. He swore lustily as he rode because the bushwhacker had given him the slip and because he strongly suspected where the man was headed. He flailed his dun's withers with the reins, urging the horse to greater and then still greater speed as he headed back to where he had left Jimmy Lee and Etta.

He saw no sign of the man who had gotten away from him during his journey, and he had almost begun to let himself hope that his suspicion was wrong when he heard the sound of a shot in the distance. He knew that it had come from the grove of trees ahead of him which was his destination.

Too late.

The words rumbled through his mind. He fought against them, refusing to believe that he was too late to save Etta—and maybe Jimmy Lee as well—and finally managed to banish them.

He rode in among the trees, drew rein, dismounted, and, with his revolver in his hand, sprinted to where he could hear the sound of voices—Jimmy Lee's and a man's—but not Etta's he realized with something close to despair.

But then he saw her. She was standing stiffly with her back pressed against a tree trunk, the fingers of both hands clawing nervously at its bark. In front of her stood the man Sutton had been trailing—the man who had earlier been trailing him and Jimmy Lee. In the man's hand was a carbine and he was aiming it at Jimmy Lee who, Sutton saw, had been disarmed and whose eyes were alternately on the carbine and on the man's face which was coarse-featured and thickly bearded.

Sutton moved silently through the trees until he was directly behind the man. Then he eased forward, intending to come up close and get the drop on him. But, as he edged closer, Etta saw him. She cried out, the sound a relieved and wordless welcome.

Her cry galvanized the man with the carbine. He spun around. The barrel of his gun came up. He grinned and quietly ordered Sutton to drop his gun or, he said, he would drop Sutton.

Sutton dropped his gun. The gunman ordered him to back up. When he had done so, the man stepped forward, picked up Sutton's gun, and thrust it into his waistband.

"He snuck up on us, Luke," Jimmy Lee blurted out. "It was my fault he got the drop on us. I never heard nor seen him coming. He threw my gun and your rifle in the brush over there."

"Do something!" Etta cried shrilly. "He's going to kill me!"

Sutton wondered what she expected a man unarmed as he was to do. He said, addressing the gunman, "I reckon you're fixing to kill her to get rid of the last witness to your killing of Grant."

Sutton was not surprised when the gunman responded with, "You got it right on the first try, Deputy." There was, after all, no reason at this point and under these circumstances for the man to bother to deny what Sutton had said. Which means, Sutton thought grimly, that Jimmy Lee and me are also going to be goners right along with Etta. He won't want to leave either of us alive either after he's admitted in front of the both of us that he's the one who murdered Grant.

"She'll be better off dead," the man growled, "than living the kind of life she's been living."

"What's that mean?" Sutton asked, hoping to keep the man talking, believing that the more time that passed without any shooting, the greater were his chances of making a move of some kind that might save them all—or some of them at any rate.

"You mean to tell me you don't know how my sister's been earning her living?" the man snapped and spat as if to rid his mouth of something distasteful.

Sutton, startled by the man's unexpected words,

turned incredulous eyes on Etta. "This here's your *brother?*" he asked her, indicating the gunman.

She dropped her eyes, nodded.

So that's it, he thought. That's why she stuck like glue to the lies she's been telling about Grant's murder. But he had to hear it from her to make himself believe she would send an innocent boy to his death to protect this killer facing him, who happened to be her brother. "You lied to cover up for him, didn't you?"

Still without daring to look directly at Sutton, Etta answered, "I had to. Ray, he's *kin.*"

"Look what it's got you," Sutton shot at her. "You covered up for a killer and now here he is all set to mow you down for your trouble."

Etta began to weep. Her hands formed into fists and pressed against her closed eyes.

"I had been looking for her for years," Ray Spode told Sutton. "When we were just tads, our parents died of influenza and we were sent to live with two different families. Mine pulled up stakes not long after and went to California. By the time I was fifteen, I left them and all the time since, no matter where I went, I kept looking for Etta. Finally I found her in Virginia City. I wish to God now that I hadn't." Spode gave his sister a look of utter and complete contempt.

"At first," he went on, "I thought it was Seth Grant who was making her live like she was living. I asked her if that wasn't so and she told me it was—that Grant had forced her into what she called 'the life.'"

"So you decided to kill Grant to rescue your sister from a life of degradation, is that it?" Sutton asked.

"Yes," Spode answered. "I thought if Grant was out of the picture she'd change. But she didn't! When I decided to go looking for her after I'd told her and the two men to skip town till after the kid was hanged, I found her in Painted Rock and she was doing the same thing all over again just like before. That's when I made up my mind to kill her like I'd already killed Rutledge—and you too, Deputy, almost—at that freighter's place I'd trailed Rutledge to."

"Ray, you can't," Etta moaned. "You can't kill your own kin!"

"You just wait and see if I can't!" Spode exploded in fury, causing Etta to shrink from him.

"But before I could kill her," Spode continued more calmly, "she gave me the slip with Tully. Well, I caught up with Tully and killed him—"

"No, you didn't," Sutton contradicted. "He died later but he was alive when I found him."

Spode waved Sutton's remark away. "But he told me Etta had left him and had it in mind to go back to Virginia City once the kid had been hanged.

"I went back to Virginia City, meaning to wait for her to show up there. I was there when you"—he indicated Sutton—"showed up and broke the kid out of jail. When I heard about that and how the sheriff was saying you were bound and determined to find Etta sooner or later and get her to tell the truth about Grant's death, I went hunting you.

"I almost had you too until you and the kid gave me the slip back along the trail. I kept after you though and finally wound up in Silver Dollar where I heard talk about how you had caught up with Etta there and were on your way back to Virginia City with her and the kid. I went after you. Maybe I wouldn't have caught up with you if you hadn't stopped for the night—but you did and I found the ashes of your fire. The rest you know about."

"It was me he was trying to shoot from that rise!" Etta told Sutton. "He told me so before you came back."

"You're fixing to kill all three of us, aren't you, Spode?" Sutton asked while at the same time directing his gaze to Jimmy Lee and giving the boy an almost imperceptible nod.

"What makes you think a thing like that?" Spode asked with another mirthless grin.

"We know the truth, the boy and me, the same as your sister here does, so it stands to reason if you intend to kill her you'll kill us too for the selfsame reason."

"You're pretty smart for a lawman," Spode remarked, still grinning and displaying his tobacco-stained teeth. He raised his carbine.

As he did so, Sutton gave Jimmy Lee another nod, trying to tell the boy to move back so that he would be out of Spode's line of sight.

Jimmy Lee, to Sutton's intense relief, did step back although Sutton could not be sure if the move had been the result of the boy having understood the silent signals he had been giving him or if it was merely of his own volition—a coincidence. Whatever the case was, Sutton was relieved to have the boy out of the line of fire if only for the moment.

Spode swung to the left, leveling his carbine at Etta. She screamed.

Spode chuckled, a deep throaty sound that resembled a bellows gone bad.

Sutton eased to his left, putting some distance between himself and Spode.

Spode's chuckle faded away as he scowled at his sister. "It's pay-up time, Etta," he muttered.

"Ray," she whispered, her voice breaking on the name. "Don't do this to me. Please don't. I promise you —I won't ever do anything bad again, not ever. I—"

"You swore to me that Grant forced you into doing what you were doing with all those men back in Virginia City!" Spode shouted at her. "You lied to me then and you're lying to me now! I'll never believe another word you say to me." Oddly, Spode's grin returned, a travesty of mirth. "You can turn your back, if you want to. That way you won't see it coming. Though you'll be sure to hear it coming."

Etta stiffened. She closed her eyes.

Sutton sprang forward just as Spode brought the carbine to his shoulder. He landed on the man and took Spode down to the ground. Before Spode could react to having been jumped, Sutton had a grip on the carbine and was twisting it out of the man's hands.

When he had the gun, he raised it, intending to club Spode with it to render him unconscious so he could tie him up. But, before he could bring the butt of the carbine down on Spode's skull, Etta ran up to them and proceeded to kick violently at her brother while cursing him at the top of her voice.

Spode grabbed her ankle, pulled on it, and she fell on top of him and Sutton.

Sutton tugged desperately at the carbine, trying to pull it free of Etta beneath whose body it was now buried. When he found he could not dislodge it, he let go of Spode and shoved Etta to one side. As she tumbled to the ground, the carbine came free. Before Sutton could use it as he had planned, Spode savagely kicked him in the groin.

Pain screamed within Sutton. He dropped the carbine and doubled up in agony.

He was barely aware of Spode's loud laughter as the man picked up the carbine and scrambled quickly to his feet. With his eyes squeezed shut in the face of the awful pain that was consuming him, Sutton did not see Spode aim the gun at him where he lay, still writhing in agony, on the ground by Spode's boots. But he did hear Spode say, "You're friskier than a cow when it's heel fly time. I'd better put you out of your misery first and then see to the other two."

Sutton stiffened, waiting for the shot that would kill him. When he heard Spode swear, he forced his eyes open and saw Etta, her arms flailing the air, racing away through the trees.

Spode set out after her. But he had not gone five paces when Jimmy Lee sprang, his hands reaching, like a panther seeking to bring down its prey.

Jimmy Lee failed to bring Spode down. For several feet, Spode ran on, Jimmy Lee clinging to him with one arm wrapped around his neck while he pummeled his head with his free fist.

Sutton commanded himself to rise. He almost screamed in the process of obeying the order because of the intense pain the effort caused him. But he managed to get to his feet and began moving as if in a pain-crazed dream as he forced himself to put one foot in front of the other, forced himself to focus not on the pain that was racking his body, awful as that was, but focus instead on the boy and the man who were linked together like some strange mistake of nature.

Just before he caught up with them, Spode gave a loud grunt, then an angry shake of his entire body, and Jimmy Lee was hurled helplessly to the ground. Sutton reached out with both hands and seized Spode by the shoulders. At the same time, he lifted his right leg and slammed his knee into the small of Spode's back, bending the man backward as he did so. He stepped back and jerked Spode toward him.

Spode fell on his back. Sutton reached down before Spode could make another move and ripped the carbine from the man's hand. Then he pulled his own revolver from Spode's waistband. He aimed his sidearm at Spode's head while tossing Spode's carbine to Jimmy Lee.

Spode stared up at him, anger in his eyes. But he did not move.

"Boy, go get the woman," Sutton ordered.

When Jimmy Lee had gone, a violent shudder ran through Sutton's body but the pain he had been feeling began to diminish. When Spode attempted to rise, Sutton put out a boot which landed squarely on Spode's chest, forcing the man back down to the ground.

Jimmy Lee returned almost immediately with Etta and his sidearm and Sutton's rifle, which he had retrieved from the brush where Spode had thrown them. "Miss Spode," he said with a smile, "just told me some good news, Luke, when I found where she was hiding from her brother."

"Good news?"

Jimmy Lee was beaming when he blurted out, "She says she can't hardly wait to get back to Virginia City so she can tell Sheriff Cobb and anybody else who'll give a listen to her that it weren't me killed Mr. Grant but her brother who did the deed."

Sutton turned to Etta who was staring down at her brother, her face a hard mask of hatred. "Is what the boy says true?" Sutton asked her.

She looked up at him. "Yes, it's true."

"How come you changed your mind about telling the truth so all of a sudden?"

"I tried all along to protect him," she said, indicating Spode. "I felt duty bound to do so though I never did like doing it the way he wanted it done. Still, I went along, as you know. And what did I get for it in the end? I almost got killed by my own kin, that's what."

Etta planted her fists on her hips as she continued to stare down at her brother who remained pinned to the ground by Sutton's booted foot. "They say, preacher men do," she continued, "that vengeance belongs to the Lord. Well, sir, not in this case." When she spoke again her voice was venomous. "Ray, I'm going to see you hang if it's the last thing I ever do on God's good green earth."

A week later, Sutton received a visitor in his room at the International Hotel in Virginia City.

He shook hands with Counselor Smythe, who had represented Jimmy Lee Cranston at his murder trial and listened as the lawyer apologized for having been out of town the previous week.

"But as soon as I got back and heard the good news, I came directly here," Smythe told him, taking an envelope from his pocket and handing it to Sutton. "I am sorry for the delay in delivering this to you."

"Better late than never, Counselor. I stopped by your office after I got back to town but your clerk told me you were representing a client in Gold Hill." Sutton opened the envelope and counted the money it held. "I think maybe you've made a mistake in the amount of money you've put in here, Counselor."

"There's been no mistake made, Mr. Sutton."

"But there's three hundred dollars in here. Maybe

you didn't hear that two of the three people you hired me to find for you were killed. The only one I was able to bring back alive was Etta Spode, so you owe me only one hundred dollars for her, not three hundred for all three."

"That three-hundred-dollar payment is one I am very glad to make, Mr. Sutton, and I do hope you will accept it in the good faith and spirit in which it is given."

Sutton hesitated a moment. Then he thanked Smythe, and when the lawyer had departed, he pocketed the money. Then he took a look in the mirror, set his hat on his head at a jaunty angle, and left his room, intending to call on Miss Letitia Parsons for the third time since returning to town.

He had almost reached his destination when he heard his name called. He turned to find Jimmy Lee Cranston running to catch up with him. When Jimmy Lee arrived breathlessly at his side, Sutton greeted him with, "How've you been keeping since last I saw you, boy?"

"I've been fine, Luke, just as fine as fine can be. I wanted to thank you for what you told the judge about what Mr. Tully told you before he died. I mean about it not being me who killed Mr. Grant. That and the way Miss Spode testified at her brother's trial about how her brother killed Mr. Grant saved the day for me."

"I read in the newspaper that Ray Spode is to hang come Monday and that the judge jailed Etta Spode for perjuring herself at your trial. The paper also said that the judge threw out the murder charge against you, which is good news to know."

"Yes, he did. I visited Miss Spode in jail and thanked her too for telling the truth about the murder at long last. She told me her brother would have hanged anyway for the murders of Mr. Tully and Mr. Rutledge so it all comes down to the same thing in the end. She's holding up pretty well, seems like. She told me not to fret about her. She asked me could I forgive her and I said I already had."

"I reckon you've been breathing a bit easier and sleeping a lot sounder lately on account of the way things have worked out."

"You bet I have, Luke."

"What are your plans for the future now that you're free as the breeze?"

"Well, I spoke to Sheriff Cobb and he told me I was a mite young yet but to come back and see him in a year or so."

"I don't follow you, boy. You spoke to the sheriff about what?"

"I taken the notion that I'd like to be a deputy sheriff the way you was. I sort of fancy the notion of going around righting wrongs the way you did for me. Course, I can't hope to be as slick at it as you was, not at first I can't."

"You put too much of a shine on what I did, boy. It was a little luck and a lot of stick-to-itiveness that pulled me through, that's all."

"You sure are a modest man, Luke. You don't even want to let on that what you did was nothing short of saving my life."

"I was glad I could be of help to you." Sutton thrust a hand into his pocket and came up with his deputy's badge. "I forgot to hand this back to Sheriff Cobb. Truth is, I've steered as clear of him as I could since I got back on account of I figured he must be mad at me for busting us out of jail."

"Oh, he was mad at you, but he's not anymore," Jimmy Lee hastily assured Sutton. "He told me he'd got over it. He even said that he understood why you did what you did."

"In that case, I intend to pay a call on him to tell him that I think you're not one day too young to be his deputy. I'll tell him how you helped me hold off that mob of Etta's men friends back in the hotel in Silver Dollar. Also about how you jumped Ray Spode and held tight to him when he went gunning for his sister, which was the only way I could have got the drop on him. Those two things alone prove to me you're man enough to be the best deputy sheriff this town ever had. You tell Sheriff Cobb I said so."

Sutton reached out and pinned the deputy's badge to Jimmy Lee's shirt.

Jimmy Lee broke into a broad smile. After shaking hands with Sutton, he headed down the street on the run.

Sutton called out to him.

When Jimmy Lee stopped and looked back at him, Sutton called out, "Considering what I just said about how you've gone and turned yourself into a man—and a brave one at that—I reckon it's about time I broke myself of the habit of calling you 'boy,' don't you?"

Jimmy Lee did the impossible. He smiled even more broadly.

About the Author

Leo P. Kelley has read and traveled widely, and his writing reflects his wide-ranging experiences. In addition to the Luke Sutton series, he is the author of several other Westerns, including *Morgan* and *A Man Named Dundee.*